PROTECTED

PROTECTED

CLAIRE ZORN

sourcebooks
fire

Published by Sourcebooks Fire, an imprint of Sourcebooks, Inc.
P.O. Box 4410, Naperville, Illinois 60567-4410
(630) 961-3900
Fax: (630) 961-2168
sourcebooks.com

Originally published in 2014 as *The Protected* in Australia by University of
Queensland Press.

Library of Congress Cataloging-in-Publication Data

Names: Zorn, Claire, author.
Title: Protected / Claire Zorn.
Description: Naperville, Illinois : Sourcebooks Fire, [2017] | Originally
  published: Australia : University of Queensland Press, 2014. | Summary:
  Nearly a year after her popular older sister's accidental death, Hannah
  meets Anne, a guidance counselor, and Josh, a potential new friend, who
  offer her the chance to move forward.
Identifiers: LCCN 2016050932 | (alk. paper)
Subjects: | CYAC: Death--Fiction. | Grief--Fiction. | Bullying--Fiction. |
  Self-realization--Fiction. | Friendship--Fiction. | Counseling--Fiction. |
  Australia--Fiction.
Classification: LCC PZ7.1.Z67 Pro 2017 | DDC [Fic]--dc23 LC record available at
https://lccn.loc.gov/2016050932

Printed and bound in the United States of America.
MA 10 9 8 7 6 5 4 3 2 1

For Marcella

ONE

I HAVE THREE months left to call Katie my older sister. Then the gap will close and I will pass her. I will get older. But Katie will always be fifteen, eleven months, and twenty-one days old. She will always have a nose piercing and a long, curly knot of dark hair. She will always think that The Cure is the greatest band of all time. She will always have a red band of sunburn on her lower back from our last beach vacation.

Forever.

The bus jolts and shudders along the street, a box of heat and sweat and BO. My fellow students flick the random spitball and hurl the occasional insult. Someone is a fat cow. Someone is going to do something filthy to someone else's mother. Someone has a thing for Ms. Thorne. There is laughter in the back, but none of it is directed at me. Nothing and no one touches me.

A fire is burning somewhere. Across a gully, gums and leaf mulch are smoldering, the eucalypt oil hissing, tree flesh twisting. The smoke drifts in a thick, putrid mass, up from the gully, over the ridge. It clings to the air, that acrid scent. It might be technically in its last month, but the Australian summer doesn't stick to the calendar rules. The heat will hang around past its welcome.

The bus heaves itself around a corner and onto my street. It was a good street to invest in, my dad said. A fire ripped through years ago and took out almost every house on this side of the gully. It scared the crap out of everyone. Prices dropped and my parents swooped. "Won't see anything like that again for a while," he had told us, meaning the cataclysmic firestorm that ate homes and schools and the community center. We were smarter than those people. Dad designed a house with fire protection: sprinklers that cast large curtains of water mist, double brick walls, heatproof glass, all that.

The people who live around this area fall into three main categories: former city dwellers, retirees, and the people who have lived here forever—raised their kids in the family home and never moved. You can tell the city people and forever families because they drive hybrid cars and have rain barrels and bird feeders in their yards. The retirees have flat squares of treeless grass in front of their homes and wash leaves off their driveways. It's weird to live in the Blue Mountains if you hate leaves so much—the place is full of trees.

A highway runs up and over the mountains, with small towns most of the way along it. Some places are popular with tourists and have cafés and boutiques and gift stores. Then there are towns like ours: we have a newsstand, a liquor store, and a bakery that sells pies I'm pretty sure are just store bought and heated up in a microwave. There's an unspoken rivalry between the upper and the lower mountains; those up at the top think that the people who live farther down are middle-class snobs and the lower-mountains residents call the ones up in Katoomba "feral hippies" or, worse, "greenies." We live midway up and my mum grew up here, so I guess that makes us middle-class-forever greenies.

The bus pulls into my stop, and I peel myself from the vinyl seat. I follow a handful of others down the aisle and off the bus. The air outside is fresher but no cooler. I walk the two hundred yards from the bus stop to my house. My elderly neighbor, Mrs. Van, is in her yard. She's of the variety that despises leaves, and she's armed herself with a rake that's bigger than she is. I

3

don't feel I have the resilience for a Mrs. Van conversation right now. Katie would have stopped. She would have stopped and chatted to Mrs. Van—not because she was a particularly chatty person but because she knew the more she talked, the more cash she would get in a Christmas card from Mrs. Van at the end of the year.

She would stand next to me in our driveway and tell outrageous lies to Mrs. Van. She once told her she was going to spend the holidays in Borneo building shelters for diabetic orangutans.

I wave to Mrs. Van and quicken my pace up the front steps.

Inside, the house is dark, curtains drawn against the heat. A floor fan whirs in the corner of the living room. Its blades make a *tick, tick* sound, like a slowly dying insect. I go down the hall. I turn the handle of her door very quietly and push it open. The carpet is soft and spotless beneath my feet. Her bed is neatly made. A selection of lilac cushions are arranged on the silver-and-white-striped comforter. Her desk is clear. Pens and pencils stand in an empty jam jar. The bulletin board on her wall remains crammed with photos and pictures torn from magazines: clothes, catwalk models, close-up shots of fabric patterns, feathers, colored glass. She was always pinning new things up. Now dust clings to the curled corners of photos. Normally, I don't touch anything, but this afternoon, I slide the top drawer open, and there, on top of notepads and

4

notebooks, is her iPod. I put it in the pocket of my skirt. Then I just stand there in the middle of her room, my backpack still on my shoulders, my heart pounding.

I close the door behind me when I leave. At the end of the hall is Mum and Dad's room. Mum is asleep on the bed, all the stuff that was piled on it—unread mail, used tissues, dirty clothes—is in a pile on the floor. I go to the kitchen to find something to eat.

My mother used to be a professional homemaker. She had a section in the weekend newspaper magazine where she would offer advice on things like how to make a festive table centerpiece out of pinecones or the perfect method for roasting a leg of lamb. She was the type of person who could take an oil drum and turn it into a decoupage side table if you gave her fifteen minutes and some craft glue. Her true passion—and she was the kind of person who used that phrase a lot—was organic, GMO-free baking; there were always some weird sort of muffins waiting for us when we got home from school, like pawpaw fruit and flaxseed or something. She'd had a book published: *The Wholefood Manifesto*. Note, a "manifesto," not a cookbook. As if she were the type to wander down to the local dairy farm and pick up a fresh pail of milk for our muesli every morning. Katie called it "The Wanker Manifesto."

Mum is no longer that person. She is like a husk from the

organic buckwheat pancakes she doesn't make anymore. She sleeps for large chunks of the day, and I am not exaggerating when I say she hasn't left the house since Katie's funeral. That was almost a year ago.

Now as I scout around for something to eat, I find that the pantry is almost empty, except for a bag of potatoes (not organic) and a couple of boxes of two-minute noodles (definitely not organic). I open the freezer; it's not much better: some meat from the butcher, still in its paper bag, and about seven almost-finished loaves of bread. I salvage two pieces, put them in the toaster, and flick through a Kmart catalog. Down the hall, the toilet flushes, and then Mum comes out into the kitchen, yawning like it's six in the morning instead of four in the afternoon.

"Hi, sweetie." She leans her hip on the counter. She has a habit of hovering around me like she's about to say something meaningful. It's terrifying. The side of her face is patterned with red marks from the pillow. The silver roots of her hair are showing. She watches me with the intensity of someone who's trying to perform a Jedi mind trick.

"How are you?" she asks.

You never know—maybe one day it will work. Maybe one day I will open my mouth and it will all come rushing out. I'll be able to tell her how I am. I'll know how I am. Not today.

"OK," I answer. I sit on a stool and continue looking through the Kmart catalog at pictures of friendly-looking people having barbecues and playing Ping-Pong.

Mum gives up watching me, sighs, and opens the fridge, which is possibly a breach of several environmental laws. The thick, sour smell of past use-by dates and rotting vegetables seeps into the kitchen. Mum doesn't seem to notice as she rifles through the shelves and pulls out a tub of yogurt. I wonder how old it is. The smell lingers after she closes the fridge.

She peels back the lid and stirs the yogurt with a teaspoon. She doesn't eat any, just stirs it around and around. She shifts her gaze to the back window and its view of the deck. On our living room wall, there is a framed photo of Katie as a toddler splashing in a wading pool on that deck. Now the deck is strewn with leaves and twigs, probably the messiest it has ever been. It's certainly not bushfire safe.

"How was school?" she asks finally. Almost absentmindedly, as if she's remembered there's something else she should probably ask me from time to time.

"Fine."

She just nods.

I leave her and go outside, down the steps off the back deck, and along the little path that leads through flower beds to the edge of the scrub. There is a large, flat rock there that juts out over the gully. Katie and I used to pretend it was a pirate ship/stage/New York apartment. I pull her iPod from my skirt pocket and turn it on. There are one thousand eight hundred seventy-four songs on it. I put the earphones in my ears and hit "shuffle all songs." First up is a song by a guy who insists repeatedly that he doesn't have a gun. I lie on my back and feel the warmth of the day's sun melt into my bones.

My father's garden languishes in the heat. He will come home later and hobble around with the hose, watering everything in the twilight. He will probably take a broom and hide a grimace as he clears the back deck and path of leaves and twigs. He won't say a word about the pain that must run rivers through his limbs. He will go inside and get his painkillers from the medicine cabinet while my mother watches television without a word.

There is a court date in six weeks' time. For the past year, the police have asked me to provide a witness statement. Dad can't remember what happened. He doesn't remember anything from that morning at all. I have heard him say to my mother that everything went black, and then he woke up in the hospital with two steel pins in his left leg, four broken ribs, and a fractured arm.

And a dead daughter.

TWO

Shoes in Katie's closet:
* Three pairs of wedges (black, red, pale blue)
* Black eight-hole Doc Martens
* Four pairs of high-top Converse Chuck Taylors, various colors and patterns
* Two pairs of sandals (one silver, one blue)
* One pair of Givenchy heels (hidden right at the back of her closet under some other stuff, which indicates they were probably stolen)

WHEN YOU'RE IN a position like mine, you get to see quite a few different counselors and everyone's very eager to offer advice. Once I saw this woman (she made me call her Dr. Wendy) who tried to hypnotize me. Dr. Wendy made me lie down, and then she started trying to get me to imagine things. She told me to envisage myself in a safe place where I felt relaxed and calm. Apparently, Dr. Wendy did tons of counseling for people who've had traumatic experiences—like being held hostage or watching their family be incinerated in a bushfire—so if there's anyone who should know that the world isn't a safe place, it's her. It seems pretty stupid to me to pretend that it is. For all I know, I could be lying there in my "safe place" and a truck could come crashing in through the wall. Needless to say, Dr. Wendy and I didn't get on like a house on fire, so to speak.

The last counselor I went to was a guy named John Butts. All I could think about the whole time was what Katie would have said to him. I could practically see her sitting next to me in his IKEA-decorated office. When he introduced himself, I pictured her with a smirk, eyebrow raised. *He's probably had a fair amount of counseling himself with a last name like that.* He was a nice enough guy—really good at looking concerned— but useless when it came to actual counseling. His favorite thing to say was "I understand," which was an acute lapse in judgment if you ask me. In my mind, Katie burst out laughing. *Do you buy that? 'Cause I can see a picture over there of him and his wife and their two smiley kids. Think he ever watched one of them get crushed to death? His baby looks like an alien by the way.*

Isn't having a counselor just paying someone to listen to your problems? A rent-a-friend? You pay them a fee to put up with you for an hour, to listen to you go on and on about yourself and not judge you for it. But they probably judge you anyway. Who's to say what they write in all those notes? People assume it's all compassionate psychoanalysis, but it's probably stuff like: self-obsessed, delusions of grandeur, poor hygiene. Boring.

I have no idea what John Butts wrote about me, but I know it was costing Mum and Dad two hundred bucks a session. Mum isn't making any money at the moment, and Dad had six months off from work. I really felt they were wasting their mortgage payments on John Butts. Mum didn't really have an opinion on the matter either way. Dad phoned my homeroom teacher.

While the parenting load might have halved as a result of Katie not being around, we are also effectively one parent down thanks to Mum's walking-dead status. So Dad has been leaning heavily on what he calls our "support network." This mainly involves a lot of phone calls to the school, specifically to my homeroom teacher, Mr. Black.

I've been in Mr. Black's homeroom since the start of sixth

grade, back when I had friends. He's the design and technology teacher—a short man with a head that is almost perfectly round and bushy eyebrows that meet in the center of his forehead when he speaks. He wears blue overalls all the time, with a ruler and pencils stuck in the front pocket, in case he's required to measure something on the fly. I think that's why Dad likes him so much. He seems to take every one of my dad's calls very seriously. The result of this Hannah-won't-go-to-counseling call was Mr. Black pulling me aside during homeroom today.

We were sitting, dutifully reading our books (He makes us read during homeroom so he can focus on sudoku.), and Mr. Black said, "Hannah, may I speak with you outside for a moment?"

A year ago, that kind of thing would have triggered a whole load of comments and wolf whistles from the class. I would have heard about it all the way home on the bus. "Hannah, what did you and Black do?" et cetera. But now there was nothing. I got up and followed Mr. Black out of the classroom. He closed the door behind him.

"Now, Hannah, as your homeroom teacher, it's my responsibility to look after your emotional well-being."

Despite the attention he gives my dad's calls, I doubt Mr. Black could look after the emotional well-being of a cactus.

"Your father gave me a call yesterday. He's a little… concerned. He informed me you don't want to see your current…"—he lowered his voice—"psychologist anymore." He said it like the fact I have had contact with mental health professionals is a classified state secret. "In the past, we've discussed the possibility of you seeing the school counselor to talk through things."

This is true. I was strongly encouraged to see the school counselor even before the accident. But I have spent most of my high school career feeling like a freak, and I never felt like confirming it by spending time in the counselor's office.

"I think you could find her helpful. Nobody thinks you should be dealing with things on your own since the loss of your sister."

I kept my eyes focused on the area near Mr. Black's shoes.

"How have things been for you socially?"

"Better," I whispered. Yes, my social life is booming now that I don't get pelted with pieces of food during lunchtime.

"Well, I'd like you to go speak with Anne. I have made an appointment for fourth period."

———

All the buildings at Saint Joseph's are sandstone, except for the one right at the back: a seventies redbrick number. It's full of asbestos apparently, so it's just used to store gym equipment, the school counselor, and the career advisor. It looks like a prison from the outside, but inside is a wide, blue-tiled stair-case that winds up five floors and a stained glass window that spans its full height. As I climbed up the staircase, it reminded me of a deep, clear swimming pool.

When Anne opened her office door, I was immediately skeptical. She had a purple woven shawl wrapped around her shoulders and looked like the kind of person who might collect crystals and use the term *spirit animal*. She smiled, held the door open for me, and told me to take a seat. The room was large and square and looked almost like a living room except there was no television. Anne sat opposite me. In the empty chair next to me was Katie. I could picture her so clearly. She was chewing gum. She looked at Anne, then at me. *Hannah, she's going to ask you what shape your pain is.* Katie widened her eyes. *What are you going to say? Is it Katie shaped? As in, totally bangin'?*

I swallowed and waited for Anne to start asking me questions. She opened the folder and took a deep breath.

"Jeez, I'm going to need a smoke after this one. Bloody hell."

Katie raised her left eyebrow.

"What class did you get out of?" Anne asked.

"Math."

"Well, I made it worth your while, didn't I?"

I smiled.

"I've got your academic record here." She said "academic record" in a funny voice, mock-posh, and held a piece of paper up, peering at it over her glasses. "You're in the top five percent for everything but math and PE. Can you find an office supply store?"

It was a weird question. "Um, yes."

"Well, go there and buy a calculator. Problem solved." She smiled. "Your grades haven't dropped off since your sister died. Clearly, there's something wrong with you."

"OK."

"I'm joking."

"OK."

"Well, I suppose you know why you're here." She spoke patiently, like she knew I had heard it all before. I looked at the patterned carpet. It was disgusting, the type they design so you won't notice if anyone vomits on it—so ugly you could understand why that might be a risk.

"You've been through something awful—actually, 'awful' doesn't really cover it, does it? Bloody hell." She glanced at her notes, raised her eyebrows. "And your dad is going to court in six weeks. You're going to be assessed by a psychiatrist and, depending on what they say, might be questioned in court. Am I right?"

I nodded.

"Because you were a witness?"

I could feel it then; it started as a pain in my chest and then I couldn't find my breath. I closed my eyes because that's the only way I can feel like I'm hidden in a small space without actually being hidden in a small space.

"Hannah? Are you OK? You've gone a bit pale. You need to open your eyes. Come on. Good. Look out the window and tell me what you see out there. Go on, tell me."

"Trees."

"What color are they?"

"Green."

"Green all over? Come on. What do you see? I need details."

I tried to focus on the window and not the feeling in my chest. I told her what I saw: the green leaves swaying on branches high up in the blue sky.

"Does that happen to you a lot? That panic response just then?"

I nodded.

"You can flick your brain out of it, but it takes practice. We'll work on it. Let's leave that alone and have a chat about your social life. Electric, I presume?"

Katie piped up. *Do you think it's ethical for a school counselor to use so much sarcasm?*

"It's fairly quiet," I answer Anne.

"Aha. Can you name the last person you were good friends with?"

I shift my attention back to the carpet.

"Oh, come on," Anne says. "You're the most fascinating person I get to talk to, Hannah. It's usually all just playground fights and teacher crushes. You're the only one keeping me awake here. Name the last person you were good friends with. That's all I want—a name. I'll leave you alone after that."

I look up.

"Charlotte."

I met Charlotte at preschool. She had white-blond hair, cut with thick, blunt bangs across her forehead. I remember that I wanted to be her friend because I liked her hair and the dress she was wearing. Things must have been pretty simple back then because I picked Charlotte to sit next to and that was that—we were best friends. I guess she must have thought my outfit was OK too.

Charlotte's mum's name was Karen, and she worked at the newsstand. She had bright-red hair, like the color of ink from a red ballpoint. She also had a Chinese symbol tattooed in the middle of her back; you could see it above the band of her jeans when she sat down. I don't know what it meant; she wouldn't tell me. I used to call her "Mrs. Burke" because that was Charlotte's last name. But one day, she told me to call her Karen and that Mrs. Burke was her mother's name. Charlotte comes across as quiet, but she isn't shy. She is just very deliberate about everything she says. She would come out with these killer one-liners that left a lot of people a little shocked. She was a useful arsenal to have nearby when Katie was around.

Charlotte and I ended up at the same primary school and in the same class, and we clung to each other in that creepy, obsessive way you do when you're little. (My mum said we were thick as thieves, and I remember I was really hurt by that because I thought she meant thick as in dumb.) Karen started working Thursday nights and Charlotte would come to my house every Thursday. It was a given that we would go to the same high school. I don't think either of our parents would have split us up for fear of inflicting some horrible trauma.

"Would you count Charlotte as a friend currently?"

"No."

"Do you have any friends at the moment?"

"No."

"How long has it been like this?"

"I don't know—a few years."

18

"Right. Your dad said you went to see a psychologist for a bit. After the accident."

"Yes."

"What was that like?"

"OK."

"Did it help?"

There is, of course, the possibility that I could lie to Anne. I could just make stuff up, keep her busy for the forty minutes of our allotted time with a wild-goose chase of invented emotional red herrings. *Why do that?* you might ask. *Can't I see that I have a wide range of problems to do with my sister, who also happens to be dead, a fact that only compounds the said problems?* Well, yeah. I know I need psychological help—everyone knows I do. But I feel that if I start talking, it's like opening a trapdoor in my mind, and all the lurking black stuff will crawl out and take over my whole brain, my whole self. And I'll never be able to shut it away again. But, of course, it is a tricky thing to fool a person with a degree in psychology. I shake my head.

"Your dad said you wouldn't talk to the psychologist much… Why was that?"

"I don't know. I didn't like him."

Anne didn't tell me that talking was the path to healing. She didn't tell me that all this was part of a special journey that would make me a strong person. She just tilted her head to the

19

side and looked as if she were waiting for me to say something else. Eventually, I did because it seemed rude not to.

"Everyone wants to know about the accident. But I can't tell them anything. I don't see how constant questions about it are going to help that." I swallowed. "Sorry."

"Who's everyone? The police?"

"Everyone. Mum, the police, my grandparents, the counselors, even my dad because he doesn't remember anything."

"You can talk to me about whatever, Hannah," Anne said. "It doesn't have to be anything to do with your sister if you don't want it to be."

I looked at the carpet. It's fair to say I spend more time studying floor coverings than most people. Anne took a plastic thing like a pen out of her pocket and sucked on it.

"See? Told you. I'm supposed to be done with ciggies in six months' time. Not likely… I'm not going to bullshit you, Hannah. Can I ask the same of you?"

I felt Katie's eyes on me.

"That I not bullshit myself?"

"Do you think that's a risk?"

I couldn't answer her.

THREE

Names my dad and Katie used to call me:

* Han
* Spanner
* Spannie
* Spanline
* Spandalous
* Spandau Ballet
* Handle
* Hands Free (mainly Katie)

MY FATHER STANDS beside me in the kitchen, peering into the open pantry cupboard. It is eight fifteen and my mother is still in bed.

"There enough bread for a sandwich? I know we're low. Nanna will be here on the weekend. She'll go shopping."

"It's fine."

"But there's no cheese, is there? Vegemite? Oh, you hate that. Er, peanut butter? Only crunchy though…"

"Vegemite is fine."

"You hate Vegemite."

"No, it's fine."

"Really? Crappy-mite?"

I take the jar from him and spread it thinly onto a buttered slice of bread.

"Oh," he says. "That was Katie, wasn't it?"

"Yeah."

"Sorry." He clears his throat. "You got enough other stuff to take? Muesli bars?"

"Yeah. It's fine."

"All right." He limps over to the table and sits down. On the radio, the announcer reminds listeners that there is a total fire ban in place for the Blue Mountains. My dad turns a page of the newspaper.

After breakfast, when Dad is in the bathroom shaving, I go into Katie's room. I slide open the top drawer of her dresser. On the left side are all her sets of bras and undies, matched up in pairs. There are three lacy, expensive-looking sets. It's clearly not my area, but they look like the kind you'd wear to make an impression. She didn't bother hiding them somewhere my mum wouldn't find them. In the middle are all her socks neatly lined up in color groups and then on the right are her sets of swimsuits: racerbacks for training, then bikinis for the beach. I take a pair of her school socks and put them on, then I slide the drawer shut and leave her room.

———————

We have assigned seating in homeroom. I bet you guessed Mr. Black would be a fan of that. Charlotte sits in the same row as me, four seats down. I mostly try to avoid eye contact and she does the same. In the seat in front of me is this guy called Josh Chamberlain. He's one of the new students from the local public school, Reacher Street High. Every year, Saint Joseph's gets an influx of students whose parents think they are better off doing sophomore and junior year here rather than Reacher Street. This year, there are fifteen new kids in our tenth-grade class. They have settled in seamlessly. It seems most people around here already know each other. (How would I know? I spend most of my time living like an elderly person: reading, watching *Miss Marple*, mourning the dead.) But the most celebrated is Josh Chamberlain. It seems he is already friends with everyone—and I mean everyone. He laughs and talks with the people usually labeled too weird, shy, or bad at team sports to be considered worthy of interaction.

Maybe it's because of his excessive social life that Josh is always late, arriving five minutes after the bell without fail. Mr. Black seems to quite enjoy this. He almost smiles with relish every time Josh saunters in and he gets to dole out some extravagant form of punishment for various offenses. The first is usually hair related. Josh has dark, collar-length hair—not strictly banned for guys at school, but if it falls past the chin, it's supposed to be tied back with a rubber band. Josh's never is, no matter how many times he gets told. Mr. Black's favorite form of retribution is to produce a nice long shiny ribbon and then tell Josh to wear it until he remembers to provide his own rubber band.

This morning, after Josh has tied up his hair in a bow and taken his seat, Mr. Black recommences his sudoku puzzle. This is the signal that we are to continue reading. I never have a problem remembering to bring a book; I learned the value of carrying one with me a long time ago. Books are especially useful if you have no one to talk to; they give the illusion that you choose not to talk to anyone, as opposed to the fact you simply have no friends. This clearly isn't a problem Josh Chamberlain is familiar with. Instead of reading, he sits there, staring into space. It's a matter of seconds before Mr. Black notices.

"Chamberlain," he says so loud everyone but Josh flinches. "Where's your book?"

"Don't have one."

"Don't have one?" he asks. "Don't have one what?"

"Don't have a book."

"I can see that, Chamberlain. The answer I'm looking for is, 'I don't have one, sir.' Right?"

"Yes."

"*Yes what?*"

Josh isn't fazed. "Yes, sir!" He gives a salute. The class laughs.

Mr. Black sighs like the effort is too much for that time of the morning. "If you have no book, Chamberlain, you'll have to do something else. And you know what that is?"

"No, sir."

"Pray. If you're not reading, you're praying. I don't care what you pray for. Perhaps you could pray that next time, you remember your book. I want you focusing on God, Chamberlain. If you so much as flutter an eyelid, I'll have you suspended."

Josh assumes prayer position, head bowed, palms together under his chin. He must notice the class's approval because he stays that way until the bell signals the end of homeroom.

As I am leaving class, I feel a tap on my shoulder. It makes me flinch. I turn around and there is Josh, holding my book, *Jane Eyre*.

"You dropped this," he says. It is the first time in almost a year that another student has looked me in the eye.

"Oh, um, thanks." I take the book from him.

"Isn't that the one where the chick gets it on with her boss?"

"Um, sort of."

"Nice." He smirks. Or maybe it is a smile. He has a dimple in his left cheek.

FOUR

Things my mother used to say:
* For goodness' sake
* Katherine, I don't think that's necessary
* If you must

Things Katie used to say:
* For fuck's sake
* whatevs
* Yes, Mum (sigh)
* Er, Dad
* Er, Hannah

I READ A statistic that said eighty percent of marriages that experience the death of a child end in divorce. Who are these people that research this stuff? Like, who exactly is benefiting from that information? We are terribly sorry to hear about the death of your sibling. Did you know your parents are now more likely to get divorced? Yeah, thanks. Helpful. I take comfort in the fact that my parents don't argue. Sure, they are hardly ever in the same room long enough to argue, but I like to think that's because my dad is a workaholic and my mum spends most of her time asleep.

My dad is an architect who wanted to design museums and galleries but now works for a public housing company. You know the type: "We don't build houses; we build dreams!" It seems that lately, building other people's dreams takes a whole bunch of time. I don't know, maybe I'm wrong. Maybe he used to work this much before Katie died. Maybe I just didn't notice because the house wasn't silent the way it is now. In a bizarre sort of way, I almost prefer being at school. At least there, I'm distracted. The hours when it's just Mum and me at home stretch out like an ocean, and I have to just put my head down and swim across it.

Now my mother stands in the kitchen at the sink with a peeler and potatoes slipping in her hands. It seems she has decided she will cook dinner tonight. Her back is to me, but

I can see the reflection of her face in the window, head bowed and tilted slightly to the left as she slides the blunt blade of the peeler. I want to talk to her. Really I do. Words flicker around at the back of my throat. I want to tell her about school, about Mr. Black and assignments and even Anne. I want to tell her something about Katie. Something about those last few moments, what happened. Because I know that's all she wants to hear.

Nothing comes out of me. Not a sound. The quiet is huge between us. Even though I know it's the quiet that makes her cry, I still can't say anything. It's usually during dinner that she starts to lose it, tears running silently down her face. Dad doesn't say anything, because really, what would you say? "It will be OK"? It won't be OK. It's never going to be OK again. When she cries like that, I don't know what to do. So usually, I just sit there and pretend I'm so deep in thought I haven't noticed the fact that my mother is slowly losing her mind right there by the refrigerator.

Now I watch her eyes in the reflection of the window. The saucepan is bubbling and shaking on the stove, and I know that if she doesn't get the potatoes in soon, all the water will boil away. She doesn't hand me a potato to peel. Doesn't ask if I got the washing in or if I have any homework. It's as if I'm not there either.

When Dad comes home, we have dinner: chops, beans, and potatoes served up on retro floral plates my mother "sourced" from a vintage market years ago. Orange pansies peeking cheerfully between the beans and potatoes. (How inconsiderate.)

"You cooked!" Dad says. "You didn't have to do that. I could have made something."

She brushes him off, setting the plates down on the table. "It's fine." And no one comments that it clearly isn't fine and hasn't been for a while.

The potato is starchy and soft on the outside but hard in the middle. Dad chops his up and covers it in dollops of butter and lots of salt. Mum looks at hers and moves it around as if she's playing chess with it.

"I'm sorry," she says.

"It's fine!" Dad nudges me. "Isn't it, Han?"

I nod and carve at the shriveled, dry flesh of the chops. Lamb. *Does its mother still look for it?* I wonder. She's probably a sausage or something herself.

About a month after the accident, Dad was standing next to Mum as they rinsed the plates and slotted them into the drawers of the dishwasher. Mum's hands shook so badly that she couldn't get one of the plates in. She swore and threw it onto the floor. The plate shattered on the tiles, the sound so loud and sudden that it made me jump. "There's supposed to be four," she said. Her voice had sounded so strange, high pitched, like she couldn't get enough air. Tears slid down her face.

Dad put his arms out to hug her, but she hit him away.

"Don't you touch me!"

———————

Mum smelled of lilac and jasmine, a new perfume Dad had given her for their anniversary. She put her clutch purse on the kitchen bench and took out a compact, flipped it open, and examined her lipstick in the mirror.

"We'll probably be home late," she said, snapping the compact shut. "The concert won't finish till eleven, then there's the drive home."

Her eyes flicked to me. She smoothed her black dress over her hips.

"Does this look OK? Do I look like an old woman trying too hard?"

"You're not an old woman. Where are you having dinner?"

She grinned. "The Opera House!"

"Nice."

She trotted over to the oven and ducked down, checking her hair in the reflection. Dad came down the hall, a dark suit, aftershave. He gave a low whistle.

"Good God, who is that gorgeous woman?"

Mum ignored him, but she blushed a little. Pretty impressive after twenty years. She held out her palm for his cuff links. He dropped them into her hand and presented her with his wrists.

"Katie in her room?" Mum asked.

"With a live band from the sound of it," Dad said. "She's supposed to be working on a history assignment."

"If she hasn't bled to death from the ears. Check that, will you, Spanner?" Mum asked brightly if Charlotte wanted to come over. "You could get pizza!" she said.

I told her Charlotte was busy. My Saturday night would be the same as it was every week: dinner, then a mind-numbing detective show on ABC. My lifestyle really was as predictable as an eighty-year-old's. I wondered what Charlotte was doing. Probably at a party somewhere, a bonfire at the beach—that was the usual thing, wasn't it? Liam Hemsworth was probably there. In fact, she was probably losing her virginity to Liam Hemsworth right at that moment.

They said goodbye to Katie and left. I opened the freezer to take out a frozen pizza, thought again, and went down the hall to Katie's room.

"Katie, you want pizza?" I shouted through the door. No reply. I shouted again, knocked, opened the door a little.

She was in front of her mirror in a tiny strapless cotton dress, both arms behind her back struggling with the zipper like a contortionist.

"You frightened me!"

"Sorry, do you want pizza?"

"No! I thought they would never leave! I'm so friggin' late!"

"You want help with that?"

She dropped her arms, exasperated, and turned away from me again. I slid the zipper up her spine. Her shoulder blades jutted from her skin like they might grow into wings.

"Where are my friggin' shoes? God. I haven't even done my hair yet." She got on her knees and started rummaging under the bed. One arm reemerged, pointed at me.

"You! You have to go and listen for the door." She stuck her head up, masses of curls falling over her face. "You have to stall him till I'm ready."

"Who? Where are you going?"

"Jensen!" she said, like it was the most obvious thing in the world. "He's going to be here any minute. Aghhh! I'm so not ready." She froze, stared at me. "Shit, they are gone, aren't they? Tell me they're gone."

"They're gone."

"Was that the front door?" She jabbed in the direction of the hallway. "Go answer it! What are you doing? Friggin' go!"

It was horrible. He smiled when I opened the door. He was about six feet, with choppy, shoulder-length hair. Not in a hippie way, more in a "when I'm not reading Hemingway, I sometimes do a bit of modeling" kind of way.

"Hey! You must be Hannah? I'm Jensen." He held out his hand. He was wearing a plaid shirt, the sleeves rolled up to the elbows. I took his hand and shook it. His fingernails were very neat. He had useful-looking shoulders, like he could throw a damsel over them if it were required. I just kind of stood there thinking about that until he asked if Kate was "around."

"Oh. Yeah. She's just…she's just running a little late. Which is funny because I'm usually the one that's running late, but Mum and Dad took forever to go and, I mean, she won't be long or anything. She just can't find her shoes, I think…" I was torn between wanting Katie to show up so I would stop talking and hoping she had somehow bumped her head and knocked herself unconscious and therefore would never come out of her room. Leaving me to make more witty conversation with Jensen. I wondered if he was a painter. Decided he probably was. Or a musician. Maybe both.

"What are you up to tonight?" Jensen asked. Still smiling. He had very white teeth. Very straight.

"Me? Oh. Um. Yeah, I'm going to some party…somewhere."

"Do you need a ride?"

"What? No! No, um, Charlotte's picking me up. My friend, Charlotte."

"No worries. We're heading up to the Gearin. There's a gig on. A mate's band."

I nodded like I knew what the Gearin was.

"Don't know if they're any good." He laughed. "Have to pretend they are either way."

"Yeah, ha! Awkward."

"OK, you can stop talking now, Hannah." Katie. Smelling of lilac and jasmine. Her hair pulled up in a loose knot. Earrings I had never seen before.

"Well, hello," Jensen said.

"Hello."

Katie looked at me with an expression that said "Your job here is done. Why are you still standing there?"

"OK. Well, see you guys," I managed. "Nice to meet you, Jensen." I sounded like our mother—or, more accurately, our grandmother.

"You too, Hannah."

Katie took his hand, led him off down the sidewalk. I closed the door. Remembered an hour later that I hadn't eaten anything and the pizza was still in the freezer.

I dream that Katie and I are in the car, our old car that got smashed up in the accident. I am driving and Katie is in the passenger seat. We move through a barren field with lions roaming around in it. The car looks like it did after the accident, crushed on the passenger side. I am afraid to stop driving in case the lions get in. Katie is talking to me about a quiz show she is going on; she wants me to ask her practice questions, but I can't concentrate because I'm too worried about the lions. I glance over my shoulder and see another Katie, dead in the backseat. Her face all made up the way it was at the funeral home.

When I wake up, my arms and legs are slippery with sweat. Sleep tries to creep back over me, and I know that if I fall back again, the dream will continue. I pinch the skin of my inner forearm. Harder, harder. I twist the piece of flesh until my eyes are wide. It's very early morning; an occasional birdcall sounds. Outside my window, the morning light is warm and milky. I get out of bed, go out into the kitchen, and fill a glass with tepid tap water. There is a coughing sound in the living room, which is when I first discover that my dad has been sleeping on the couch. He must sense me enter the room because he opens his eyes, stretches, frowns at me.

"Jeez, you're up early, Han," he says, rubbing his face.

36

"Why are you sleeping out here?"

"What? Oh, ah, couldn't sleep. Didn't want to keep your mum awake tossing and turning all night."

"I was just going to watch some TV. But if you want, I'll just go back to bed."

Dad shakes his head. "No, no, you're all right. Go ahead. I'm gonna take a shower." He gets up slowly, using his arm to brace himself against the back of the couch. It's the moment any normal person would offer help, take his arm while he steadies himself. I don't. I can't. I pretend I don't even notice the obvious pain he is in. I think both of us prefer it that way.

FIVE

Names the Clones called me:
* Pig dog
* Lesbian
* Lesbefriends
* Han the man
* Smart-ass bitch

PE. My own personal hell. My reasons for hating PE are far too many to list here, but you can probably guess the basics: the uniform, the locker room, the fact that on dry land I have the coordination of a brain-damaged three-legged baby cow.

I've hated PE since kindergarten, when we had to do a ridiculous exercise called "the barrel." The teacher would stand this big plastic barrel up and the kids would gather around it, holding it to keep it steady. Then each kid, one at a time, would be put in the barrel. The idea was you had to try to get back out by somehow climbing up the sides and hoisting yourself out of the top. You did this while the others laughed and occasionally pinched the backs of your hands while the teacher wasn't looking. The whole thing seemed designed to torment students rather than actually teach them anything. Like, at least if you don't learn anything else at school, if you ever get trapped in a barrel, you'll know how to get out. I understand that it was supposed to be fun and character building or something, but when I was five, the whole barrel exercise was scary to the point where I never wanted to go to school on PE day.

Ten years later, I still get the same twist in my stomach at the start of every PE class, when we all have to sit on the basketball court while the teacher reveals what variety of humiliation we are about to be subjected to. Judging from the darkly familiar shape of the equipment bags that lie before us, it seems today's special treat is cricket. I pray my team will be fielding.

"Listen up, guys!" Ms. Thorne bellows. "There's some information you need to hear about next week's schedule."

Farther along from me sit Tara Metcalf and Amy Brooks. They both wear tiny shorts that blur the line between underwear and outerwear and sit with their legs outstretched so the guys can get a really clear view. They are discussing how pale they are despite both of them having smooth, golden skin.

Ms. Thorne stops talking and looks at them pointedly. They are oblivious.

"Amy, Tara, is there something you'd like to share?" Ms. Thorne is about five feet tall and the color of a nicely roasted chicken. She used to be a sprinter and was headed for the Olympics until an injury forced her to retire to teaching. That's how the story goes anyway. Tara especially likes to ask her lots of questions about her sprinting career, punctuated loudly with comments like, "Wow, ma'am, you must have been really fit before you were a teacher. Like, you must have been a lot skinnier before."

Now Tara smiles and says, "Sorry, ma'am!" in a singsong voice.

Ms. Thorne narrows her eyes but continues. "The swim meet is coming up in six weeks' time," she says.

No, no, no, no.

"You will all be swimming. Starting next week, we will be heading to the pool to train. I'll have the sheet then, so you can sign up for your events."

I will not be heading to the pool to train. They can expel me; they can do what they like. But I will not be heading to the pool.

And here I was thinking I'd never have to get out of that barrel again.

We grouped up at the end of the lane, caps and goggles off, hair slick from the water, steam playing on the pool surface. Our coach called out the names of people who'd improved their personal best times at that morning's training session. For the first time in six months, my name was on the list. Katie wrapped her slippery fish arms around my neck and jumped on my back. "Span-nah! Smashing it."

Later, in the locker room, she was as effortless as usual getting ready for school. She stood in her bra and undies, talking to the other girls by the fogged-up mirror. Her long hair hung over one shoulder and she untangled it with her fingers. I retreated to a toilet stall, towel wrapped around me, to change into my school uniform.

I don't know how we could have come from the same parents. Katie never appeared to try. She could wear a garbage bag and it would look like a well-executed fashion statement. I, on the other hand, was usually running late because I had spent fifteen minutes trying to get my hair right, as if going to school with a different hairstyle would change everything. Like they would turn their heads and stare at me as I walked down the hallway. *My God*, Tara Metcalf would think. *How could I have not noticed how unbelievably cool Hannah McCann is? Look at her incredibly awesome hair!*

Once dressed, I ventured out of the toilet stall and started to fix my hair. I was almost satisfied with it and halfway believing I might just make it through the day without an incident when Katie stopped her conversation and sighed in a way that was more a performance than it needed to be.

"Step away from the hairbrush, Hannah. Am I going to have to confiscate it?"

She strode over to me, wrestled the brush from my hand, and threw it—a little melodramatically in my opinion—over her shoulder. She pushed my head forward and proceeded to violently mess up my hair.

"Got to admit," she said, "I can understand why you struggle with this." She pulled my head back again, took a rubber band from her wrist, and performed a quick, complex movement, which resulted in my hair being anchored in a messy knot on the top of my head.

"There."

"Now I just look like everyone else."

She patted me like you would an obedient dog. "Exactly."

The others trickled out of the locker room until it was just Katie and me. She leaned over the basin, mouth slightly open and applied mascara to her long eyelashes.

"How's Jensen?" I asked her in my most carefully casual voice.

"You tell Mum and Dad about him and I will kill you. I will. In your sleep probably."

"Obviously. He's not in school, is he?"

"No, Hannah, he's not in school. He's nineteen."

"Nineteen?"

"Shhh!"

"He's nineteen?"

"Yeah. He's nineteen."

"What? Is he at college?"

"Yes. Modern American literature. Or something."

I knew it. I laughed. "What do you talk about?"

She gave me a look. "Some of us don't have to spend all our time talking."

———

The short walk home from the bus stop feels like a marathon in the oven-dry air. There is the distant sound of sirens on the highway. I let my shoes scuff on the asphalt and watch the little gray pebbles scatter. A car turns onto our street, and I feel it approach and slow down, the pulse of music thudding from the stereo. I look over expecting it to be someone who just got their driver's license. But it is my grandmother's pink hatchback. She stops next to me, lowers the window. The throaty wail of Dolly Parton floats from her car: "Jolene! Jolene!"

"Hannah!" As if she should be the one to be surprised to see me. "In you hop." It is literally fifty yards to my house. "Come on!"

I walk to the passenger door and get in.

She reaches over and turns down the stereo. "How about this dreadful heat! It's a disgrace," she says, as if there is someone to be blamed. I notice the backseat laden with grocery bags.

"Thought I would drop some things off. Help your mum out. Was going to come Saturday, but your dad said…" She waved her hand instead of using words to finish.

Over the past few months, Nanna has made a habit of randomly turning up with groceries and doing things around the house, like cleaning the bathroom and vacuuming. At first she was nothing but warm and supportive toward my mother. But at some point, the expiration date for accepted grief passed and Mum's behavior has slipped from natural to indulgent in Nanna's eyes. She's troubled that our house hasn't returned to its former *Vogue Living* standard. My mother has lost her passion for finding the perfect throw cushion, and to Nanna, this is equivalent to losing the will to live. Her remedy is frozen meals and Mr. Clean.

In case it isn't obvious, Nanna is my mother's mother. I have no idea how old she is since her appearance hasn't changed in my lifetime. I have never seen a gray hair on her head or her fingernails unpolished. She is the kind of person who takes other people's lack of grooming as a personal affront. There is nothing that can't be achieved, in her opinion, with the right hairstyle and a well-ironed pantsuit.

She turns into our driveway and parks the car. She looks over at me, lips pursed.

"Well, how is she?" Meaning my mother.

"The same."

Nanna sighs and opens her door. "Have you had your colors done yet?" she asks, referring to the gift certificate she got me for a session with a color consultant whose job is to tell you what season your complexion is and how to dress accordingly. Nanna is evangelical in her attitude toward the practice.

"No."

"You should—it will make a world of difference."

Inside, the house is as quiet as if it were empty. Nanna bustles past me and down the hallway.

"Yoo-hoo! Paula!"

"She might be asleep, Nan," I say. But then this possibility is the very reason Nanna is here.

She lets herself into Mum's bedroom and I hear Mum raising her voice. I start unpacking the groceries. A few minutes later, Nanna reemerges.

"She's not doing anyone any favors carrying on like this," she mutters. She pulls a bottle of disinfectant from the cupboard and heads for the bathroom.

I should point out that Nanna isn't intentionally callous. It's not that she doesn't mourn for her eldest granddaughter. Nanna adored Katie. She loved her sharp remarks and her attitude and the fact that she carefully plucked her eyebrows. But she believes in proactivity as if it were a religion. It's like she has decided that crying is a waste of time because it won't achieve anything. Or maybe her grief is an energy that she just doesn't know how to deal with, so she has channeled everything into getting Mum back on track.

When the bathroom is presumably back to hospital standards of cleanliness, Nanna raps sharply on my bedroom door and lets herself in. She finds me sitting on the floor, reading.

"That a schoolbook?" she asks, suspicion in her voice.

"Um. No."

She raises her left eyebrow. "Do you have homework?"

"Not really."

"You're not a very good liar, Hannah."

"Sorry."

She throws a small pink box onto my bed. "I got you those. Waxing strips. For your legs. You'll find it better than shaving."

It's that—not Katie's photos or her empty bedroom or the spare seat at the dinner table—it's that small moment that pulls a lump into my throat.

SIX

Items I needed to replace after high school started:
* School shirts (x 4)
* Backpack (stolen)
* Pencil case (vandalized)
* Phone (screen smashed)

THE FRUIT IS bullet hard and bursts in a cold fright between my shoulders. It is lunchtime, I am on my way to my spot when it hits me, and the shock of it halts me there in the middle of the school yard. I turn around in time to see Josh's face freeze when he realizes he's hit the wrong target. There are a few laughs and then silence. Tara and Charlotte are standing not far away, talking to an eleventh grade guy. Tara's mouth drops open and she tries to stop herself from laughing. Charlotte just looks worried. I stand there stunned for a few seconds. I feel my stomach turn and my pulse starts to thud in my temples. I turn and walk quickly to the outdoor toilets. Everyone's eyes are on me, but no one says a word. I rush into a stall and lock the door behind me as all my breath escapes from my lungs. I close my eyes and crouch down low to the ground. Soon the bell rings, signaling the end of lunch break, and I hear the babble of voices and feet shuffling as everyone else moves on the current to third period. But I am stuck, caught there, crouched low with my knees to my chin as I feel the juice seep through my white shirt. Eventually, I reach around and touch the goo on my back. It is a plum, I'm pretty sure. My history class is probably starting a discussion on the downfall of the Russian Empire. But I can't move.

There are footsteps. "Hannah? Hannah? It's Ms. Thorne." Her voice is on the other side of the door. "Charlotte said something happened. Are you OK? I'm here with Anne, the counselor. Sweetie, there's no one else here. Can you open the door? We just want to help you out. Are you OK?"

"I'm OK," I whisper.

I hear Anne. "Hannah, we just need to see that you're OK. Otherwise, I might have to kick down the door and I'm not sure I'm up for that. I've got my good shoes on."

My legs wobble as I stand. I turn the lock on the door and let it swing open.

"Good work, Hannah," says Ms. Thorne.

Anne puts her hand on my shoulder. "Come up and have a chat?"

I nod.

She makes me a cup of tea. "Chamomile," she says. "French for *camel piss* because, let's face it, that's what it tastes like. Better for you than caffeine though."

I sip the tea.

Anne sits down. "What happened?"

Katie is there, of course. *Yeah, Hannah, tell her. Because from my perspective, a cute guy giving you any kind of attention has got to be a good thing.*

I can't get my breathing right. I close my eyes.

"Hannah, can you open your eyes? Look at that picture on the wall. Tell me about it."

I can't get the information from the picture to translate into words.

"You don't even have to use a sentence. Just list what you see."

"Blue, um, water, sky, sand."

51

"OK. Can you take a slow breath in while I count? One, two, three, four, five. And out for five."

She counts and I try to do what she says.

"We're going to do that three more times."

I breathe while she counts, and I can feel the fizz behind my forehead settle.

"You were having a panic attack, Hannah," she says. "It's OK, there's nothing wrong with you. That's what we're pro-grammed to do when we feel threatened, basic flight-or-fight response. It's the reason humans still exist. It stopped us all from getting eaten by saber-toothed tigers. That's why you get chest pain, an increase in heart rate, feel tingly in your arms and hands—it's the blood moving to your muscles so you're ready to run. That's all."

"OK."

"You can override it. Next time, I want you to take a few minutes and keep your eyes open if you can. Then you need to take some very slow, deep breaths—breaths right into your diaphragm. Here." She lays her flat palm on her stomach and closes her eyes. "When you breathe in, you should feel your hand move. That's your diaphragm pushing your stomach out. That controlled breathing is going to help switch the adrena-line response off, help you think more clearly. Stop the panic.

"I have to do a few things in my office. I'm going to let

you sit here and practice slowing that breathing down." She disappears for about ten minutes and then comes back with an armful of manila folders. She sits down and starts sorting through them, putting piles on the floor.

"Can I ask what you like to do? Any hobbies?" She keeps her focus on the folders, as if it's just a casual conversation and she's not going to analyze my response.

"There's nothing really. Anymore."

"What did you used to like to do?"

I swallow. "Swim."

"Good. Where do you like to swim? Ultimate destination: beach or pool?"

"Either. Anywhere. I just… I like being in the water."

"Have you been swimming lately?"

I close my eyes and shake my head.

"No, Hannah. Open your eyes. Come on, stay with me. Open them."

I take a deep breath and do as she tells me.

"We don't have to talk about that. We'll come back to it. What else do you like to do?"

I shrug my shoulders, and she smiles and shrugs her shoulders back at me.

"What's something you do a lot?"

Another deep breath. "I like to make lists."

Anne widens her eyes. "Ooh good. What do you make lists of?"

I look at the carpet. "Just…stuff."

"Stuff, huh?"

"Do you think it's a problem that I do that? Like, is there something…wrong with me?"

"No, I don't think there's something wrong with you. Do you make lists obsessively? Like, are you always listing things in your head? Do you feel anxious and making lists is the only thing that makes you feel better?"

I shake my head.

"Then it's probably a good thing. Maybe it's helping you process things."

"OK."

"Now. It's going to be the end of the period soon. I'm going to go and find you another shirt from lost and found. Your job is to sit here and breathe. Then, when you feel ready, you can go to your next class, OK?"

I agree because I know, today, it won't get any worse. And I am right. When I walk into biology class, Tara looks up, but no one says a word about me. No one hands me a note with a drawing of something obscene. No one even makes a comment about me being in the girls' toilets with Ms. Thorne.

Later, my dad pulls the shirt out of the laundry basket and holds it at arm's length.

"Han? What happened?" he asks.

It's the first time something like this has happened since Katie died.

"It was an accident."

That is true. It was an accident. The fruit wasn't meant for me.

"Did someone do this? Did something get thrown at you?" He looks at the shirt. "Obviously someone threw something at you. Who? Who was it?"

"Just some guy… He didn't mean to hit me."

"I thought school was going OK."

"It is. It's nothing, Dad. It was an accident."

I WISH I could rewind and start high school again, go back and do things differently—just small, seemingly insignificant things. Details. I'm not talking about what happened to Katie either. The worst thing that could happen would be for my life to go back to how it was before Katie died. That fact is a horrible, silent thing that hangs in my head and seeps into everything like thick black silt.

Before the accident, it was almost every day that I'd have to sneak into the laundry room and scrub food or pen marks from my shirt. I would tell Mum I got paint on them in art class.

But there's always someone at the bottom of the pile, isn't there?

From the moment you walk through the front gates of a school, you are judged. Assessments of your worth are made by your peers, and once they are made, you can't shift them. We are meat-eating pack animals, we humans. The weakest are identified, and when food is scarce, they are the first to be eaten by their peers.

Both Katie and Mum gave me a pep talk the night before I started high school. Mum was first. She sat next to me on my bed.

"Hannah, I know you're nervous, but you have to think of this as the first part of a wonderful adventure."

She handed me a flat square box. I opened it and inside was a scrapbook that she'd covered in vintage floral fabric. She'd screen printed "School Days" on the front cover. On the first page, in her florid handwriting, were the words: "The best person you can be is yourself." I didn't know there was an alternative. Each blank page had a stamped border, ready for me to fill with wonderful memories of high school.

She put her arm around me. "I still keep in touch with my

high school friends. Everything you need, you will find in here." She pointed to my heart. "You just have to be willing to give. So proud of you, honey."

Next up was Katie. She closed the door after Mum left.

"Hannah. You have to know it's not personal, right? But from the time we leave the house in the morning until we come home in the afternoon, I don't know you."

"What? Why?"

She sighed and rolled her eyes. "Because, you will be a fresh-man, as in automatic loser. Like, total toxic dweebsville loser. I have worked hard to establish myself, and I don't need you coming and screwing it all up. Like I said, it's not personal. Oh, and when you get to school, first thing you need to do is roll your skirt at the waistband to make it shorter. And make sure you shave your legs and pits."

"But it's blond hair, Katie. You can't even see it."

"It's not negotiable." She handed me a razor.

I didn't know how to do it. I certainly didn't know you were supposed to wet your skin and use soap to lather it up. So I stood in the middle of my bedroom and dragged the razor over my dry skin. I nicked the back of my ankles, the back of my knees, the front of my knees. Bright-red blood trickled down my pale legs. Fighting tears, I blotted at it with tissues and my skin got all raised and bumpy, so it looked like I had a horrible rash.

Mum drove Charlotte and me to school the next day, partly for the ceremonial aspect, partly because I spent the night throwing up with nerves. (Katie refused to come with us, saying she didn't want people to know we were related.) Mum stopped in the crowd of cars in front of the school. There were parents fawning over their kids like they were marching off to war. She jumped out, holding the camera, and made us stand in front of the gates while she took multiple pictures from various angles before she let us go.

Despite our best efforts to appear as sophisticated as possible, the damage was already done by the fact that, as Katie predicted, my skirt was about a foot longer than everyone else's (it did mostly hide the disaster that was my legs, however) and my backpack made me look like a turtle. My dad had insisted that I buy the official school backpack with its fifteen pockets and night-safe reflector patches. (Did it never occur to the designers that school finished at three in the afternoon?)

I plastered on a smile and waved to Mum as she drove away.

"I need to go to the bathroom," I said.

Charlotte must have heard the waver in my voice because she put her arm around me and steered me toward the girls' toilets. I left my backpack with her and went inside. The smell of body spray was so strong it stung the back of my throat.

There were girls clustered around the mirror, straining and leaning over each other, fixing their hair, smearing gloss over their lips. One of them was tall with long blond hair like in a shampoo commercial, and she looked over at me when I walked in. That was the first time I met Tara Metcalf. It's actually stupid to say that I met her, because meeting someone is supposed to mean you introduce yourselves in a civil sort of manner. Tara didn't introduce herself—she just looked at me as if I were some kind of alien that she found both repulsive and really uncool.

I went into a stall and rolled my skirt the way Katie had told me. When I came out, Tara and a girl with a pixie haircut were talking to Charlotte. It's worth pointing out that Charlotte didn't have to shorten her skirt because her mum had a way better idea of what was cool than mine. She'd also given Charlotte more detailed leg-shaving instructions. Charlotte was smiling and laughing like they were the friendliest people she had ever met.

"Oh, Hannah! There you are," she said. "This is Tara and Amy."

Tara and Amy both made a face that looked as though they were trying to smile while someone was stabbing them with hot pins. They turned back to Charlotte and kept talking like I wasn't even there. I didn't know what to do, so I just stood next to Charlotte like some stupid, loyal pet and waited for them

59

to finish. Luckily, the bell rang. I picked up my backpack and made to leave; Charlotte kept talking with them.

"Um, Charlotte," I said. "We should probably go. There's that assembly thing and…"

Tara, who was midsentence, paused and turned to me.

"Is that your bag?" she said, looking at my backpack like it was a dead animal that I had picked up and thrown over my shoulder.

"Yeah."

"Oh," she said. Amy started giggling.

Tara looked down at my legs. "Oh my God! Gross! Have you got scabies or something? Amy, look at her legs!"

"Um, no," I said. "It's just from shaving."

Amy was in hysterics by this point.

"Yeah, sure," said Tara. "Good luck with that."

Tara Metcalf was crowned queen of class that first day. She climbed to the top of the pile by scaring the crap out of all the other girls. She barely had to say anything to do it—she just flicked her hair and looked you up and down or asked questions like, "Is that how you do your hair?" and "Don't you wear deodorant?" That kind of thing. Girls who were lesser variations of her own appearance became her "friends": an army of perfectly preened Tara Clones. Everyone else was either ignored or subjected to random acts of cruelty in order to set an example to anyone who dared challenge her reign.

Despite all that, I wasn't worried about Tara. I figured I would just keep out of her way and maybe get the hem of my skirt raised. I didn't care what Tara and her little posse thought about me. I had Charlotte.

SEVEN

IN BACK OF Saint Joseph's, behind D building, is an agriculture plot. The agriculture students have to change into overalls and rubber boots for class because they spend their time mending fences and chasing the small herd of goats the school has bred. (A very useful life skill to have, I'm sure.) There's one building with a classroom and another storeroom that houses an egg incubator and textbooks about crop rotation. A porch wraps around the building, and it is the perfect place to have lunch. I sit there unseen, except for the goats, who peer at me occasionally, shuddering nervously if I make a sudden movement.

I have a very direct and discreet route from the science labs across to the agriculture plot. Technically, students are not supposed to be at the agriculture plot unsupervised, definitely not at lunchtime. But it is one of the few hidden places that the Clones haven't colonized for smoking.

I am aware of someone walking right next to me, but I keep my eyes firmly ahead until he speaks. "Hey, Jane Eyre."

I don't know what to do. I glance at him and keep walking.

"Can I have a word?" Josh ducks in front of me, walking backward to keep a few steps ahead of me.

"OK."

"Can you slow down?"

I slow.

"I want to apologize. For the fruit. Totally didn't mean to hit you."

"That's OK."

"You are literally the last person I would want to hit with fruit. There are so many other people who are more fruit-hit worthy than you."

"OK."

"Good. Where you going?"

"Nowhere."

"You walk pretty fast for a girl who isn't going anywhere. You going to sneak a smoke?"

"No."

"Nice try, Jane Eyre. I know your type—smart, quiet, smokes like a chimney. All right, well, I'll see you around. Take it easy."

And with that, he wanders off toward the cafeteria.

In the afternoon, I get home and my mother is sitting on the couch—an island in a sea of paper: junk mail, pizza coupons, bills, the local newspaper (complete with a fascinating headline about a "monster mushroom" the local dentist has found in his backyard). She is examining a letter from the lawyer's office. I recognize the letterhead. After a while, she notices me standing there and looks up, her expression like I'm another piece of paperwork that needs tending to—and I've jumped the line.

"Um, I was wondering, were you going to go to the supermarket at some point? It's just, we're kind of low on a few things…food and stuff. Nan bought some, but there's stuff we need."

She looks like she can't quite remember what food is. "Grab my purse. You can buy your lunch at school tomorrow."

"Yeah. They don't really sell toilet paper in the cafeteria, Mum. Sorry…"

She looks down at the piles of paper around her and I'm nervous she's considering them as a viable toilet paper substitute.

"You can get the bus to the stores near Johnson Street." Her voice faults a fraction over the street name. "I'll give you some money."

And once again, my lifestyle merges ever closer to that of an eighty-year-old's.

———————

At four in the afternoon, the sun is no weaker than it was at noon. I wear a sweater anyway. It's a habit I have, like an extra layer of protection between me and the world. There is the faint smell of charred eucalyptus on the breeze. A controlled burn probably. All those tiny bush creatures incinerated in place of our homes. Better to be safe than sorry.

The bus is suitably filled with a handful of grandmas. They all sit in the front, clutching the seat handles, umbrellas in hand in case the sky should suddenly change from searing blue and inflict a nasty surprise on us all. Nanna used to take us on bus trips to the shopping center near her house. Katie and I never caught buses on our own before high school, and the whole experience was as exciting as the shopping center itself. Nanna would give us each a handful of coins, which we would dutifully hand to the driver as we delivered our well-rehearsed line: "One child to Eastways Shopping Center please." My coins were always slippery in my palm by the time they got to the driver.

Katie rarely gave Nanna any trouble. When Mum came to collect us from Nanna's, she would ask quietly, "How was Katie?" and Nanna would reply that she was an angel and she didn't know what Mum was always going on about. Later, Katie would proudly empty her pockets and show me all the stuff she had stolen from Kmart.

The bus stops at the Johnson Street intersection. I can see where someone has tied a bunch of fresh tiger lilies to the telegraph pole on the corner. I have no idea who keeps doing that.

The supermarket is clogged with the usual after-school crowd: elementary school kids eating frozen Popsicles, mums pushing shopping carts filled with groceries, teenagers using the magazine aisle as a library. I spend what feels like hours in front of the cheese section, trying to remember if it's cheddar we usually get or colby. Then there're the tons of brands to choose from. Seriously, you could spend days in here just trying to decide on a block of cheese. I end up picking one at random because it seems easier and continue to inch along the dairy aisle toward the next challenge: milk.

And then I see them, right in front of me, and it's too late to turn around or duck past like I haven't noticed. Tara is holding a carton of chocolate milk; she seems to be assessing the nutritional content. Charlotte sees me first and I recognize the brief moment of panic on her face before she manages to open her mouth.

"Hi, Hannah."

Tara looks up from the milk. "Oh. Hi, Hannah."

"Hi."

There is an awkward pause.

"Hey, there's a party at Jared Marsh's this Saturday. You know Jared? You should totally come. You on Facebook? I'll message you the deets," Tara says.

Beneath my sweater, a line of sweat runs down my back. "No. I'm not on Facebook anymore."

"Oh. Well, I'm sure Char still has your number."

"I changed my number a while ago."

"Oh yeah. Ha."

I push the shopping cart past them, continue down the aisle.

"Well, see ya then, Hannah."

I end up going home with a block of cheese and a pack of toilet paper.

"How do you feel about them?" asks Anne the next day.

"Nothing. I don't know."

"You didn't feel anything? God. I'd want to scratch their eyes out."

That's what I'd do, says Katie.

"Yeah. I don't know. Charlotte…" I don't finish.

"Charlotte?"

"I know she feels bad. About everything that's happened."

"What was it about her that makes you say that?"

"I just…I know her really well. Knew her. I can tell. She gets this kind of frozen look around her eyes, like she doesn't know what to say or do. I just… We were very close for a long time."

"Like sisters?"

"Yes."

"That must be very hard on you, knowing that here is a person who would have been your refuge, your support before, and now she's not there for you. What did you feel in your body?"

"Nothing… I don't know. Sick, I guess."

"Did you feel like you did the other day? When the thing with the fruit happened?"

"No."

"Why, do you think?"

"They can't hurt me anymore. It's all stopped. It's not like it was before Katie."

69

EIGHT

Items found in Katie's drawer in the bathroom:

* Waxing strips
* Three razors
* My Little Pony Band-Aids
* Cosmetics, including five Mac eyeshadows and a Chanel lipstick that I suspect were stolen
* Eyelash curler
* Hair straightener
* Tweezers
* Mouthwash
* Dental floss

Items found in Katie's secret hollowed-out book:
* Condoms

Ms. THORNE HAS given us all permission slips to take home and have signed by our parents. It's the usual legal formality, a bit of paper that says if I drown at the pool, my parents won't hold anyone to blame but themselves. That's unlikely—both the drowning and the blame, I mean. The permission slip is still in the pocket of my backpack, and I have avoided it the way you might avoid radioactive material. The consequences of mishandling it could be catastrophic. I haven't been to a pool since Katie died.

Dad started us both swimming when we were toddlers. He said we McCanns were built for it, with our long limbs and big feet. Katie was thirteen months older than me, so she started swimming lessons first. She taught me how to do handstands in the water and curve my body in somersaults, belly up. She told me stories of kids that had been sucked into the pool filter and had limbs devoured by creepy crawlies. By the time I was old enough to start lessons, she'd already taught me freestyle and I got advanced up a level.

I followed her onto the team as soon as I was old enough. Swimming made sense to me. The rhythm of freestyle was as natural as walking. I felt at home with water rushing past my ears and an ache climbing in my legs from the kicking. It's a strange, quiet, isolated space to be in—cocooned in the water. Solitary. Meditative. Just you and the water and a clock. There's something kind of anonymous about it. No one but the coach is watching you. Not like a team sport, where the subs are on the sideline watching, heckling everything you do, pointing out every mistake you make.

I like the discipline of swimming, the control you have to have. You can't be too desperate for the next breath—if you rush it, everything gets screwed up, goes out of kilter; your stroke gets shorter, sloppier. It's all about patience, controlling that feeling that if you don't inhale immediately, you will die.

I don't think that's what it was like for Katie. I think for her, it was a game that she was very, very good at. Coach said she had an economical stroke, the smallest amount of effort for the best result. Her name got written on the team records board. She did regionals, then states, then nationals. I did regionals and states—and nationals once. Mum and Dad were pretty good about it. They tried to give us equal encouragement, and they made a fuss about my red ribbons and silver medals. I didn't really care that she was better at it than me. That wasn't why I kept it up. There was no one else from my grade on the team. I was left alone other than when Katie would joke with me. There in the pool, with both our heads under the water, was the closest I ever got to her.

I don't want to be anywhere near a swimming pool, especially not in school.

I sit opposite Anne, my rent-a-friend, in the period before lunch.

"How are you today?" she asks.

I reach into my pocket and retrieve the permission slip from Ms. Thorne. I unfold it and hand it to Anne.

"I can't go to swimming practice. Can you make my appointments with you at the same time as PE class for the next month?"

"Why? I thought you liked swimming?"

"I can't…"

"Okaaay. Remember the very first time I saw you, Hannah? I asked you one thing. Remember?"

She waits, but I don't say anything.

"I asked that you not bullshit me."

I suck my lip in between my teeth. Swallow.

"Hannah?"

"I can swim. I'm a good swimmer. I used to be on the team…with Katie."

"Aha. So you don't want to swim because it reminds you of Katie?"

I nod.

"And you don't want to remember?"

"No."

"Because to you, remembering is dangerous."

I don't say anything.

"Look, I can do that for you. I'll organize it. But I need to talk to you about something. How do you feel about the court date coming up?" She checks her notes, even though I'm sure she doesn't need to. "It's in about a month. How do you feel about maybe being questioned?"

"I don't really feel anything about it. I mean, I still don't remember what happened…"

"Yes, that's why they're going to order a psychiatric assessment—so they know you're telling the truth."

"Do you think I'm lying?"

"No, Hannah. But they need to know for the sentencing. They're not going to be as…gentle as me. Sometimes, we block out things that are traumatic—"

"I hit my head. I don't remember." I know my voice is going all high-pitched crazy-person style, but I can't help it.

Anne holds up her palms. "I want you to know that you are safe in here, Hannah."

I stare out the window at the treetops, leaves utterly still, not a breath of breeze. "You don't understand," I whisper.

"Then maybe you should help me understand."

———————

The days drift by, nothing marking one from the other until Saturday arrives and breaks the rhythm of school. I sit on the top step of the back deck. Nine o'clock and the concrete beneath my bare feet is already warm. My father stands watering the garden, protected from the sun to the point of obsessive beneath his UV-proof long-sleeve shirt and Cancer Council–approved wide-brim hat. I have skin like his—ivory white. Katie's was a few shades darker. Sun makes me burn; it made Katie glow.

When I saw her for the last time, her forehead and left temple were smothered in thick makeup like plaster to cover the injuries. I had never seen a dead person before. Her stillness was horrible and unnatural, and I wanted to grab her shoulders and shake her. "Enough, Katie! You have our attention!"

They said she was at peace. "They" being the people who nod compassionately when you hand them the check to pay for the satin-quilted white casket. Like it makes any difference what you bury her under the ground in.

———————

My dad used to whistle when he was gardening. He is quiet now, face set in concentration. Every now and then, he glances in my direction, as if he is checking I'm still there. His movements are stiff. He won't last much longer outside; then he'll go in and have some painkillers, listen to the radio, read the paper.

I hear the sound of the doorbell from inside the house. My mother answers the door just as I get there. I didn't even know she was awake. On the doorstep is Mrs. Van, our neighbor. She is holding a baking pan and wearing her Big Banana amusement park T-shirt.

"Boterkoek," she announces. It is a Dutch specialty, a dense, crumbly cake that basically tastes like a giant piece of shortbread. She brings one regularly: a cake and a reminder about God. Most people avoid talking about the serious stuff and stick to small talk, like they are afraid that if they mention the accident or Katie, we'll start crying uncontrollably and they won't know what to do. People, I have discovered, will do anything to avoid awkward situations. This involves using phrases like, "It must be almost a year since you lost your sister." As if she jumped the fence and ran away like a restless pet. Mrs. Van is the opposite.

My mother sighs.

Mrs. Van thrusts the pan toward her.

"Mrs. Van, we don't need cake. OK? Thank you." Mum starts to close the door.

Mrs. Van wedges her foot in the way. "It is a small kindness. Kindness comes from God. God told me to bring you boterkoek, and I have done this. You must not reject God when he offers you a kindness."

"God can f…fob off."

"You don't want God to fob off. Your daughter is dead. You need God."

"Thank you, but I don't need to be told what I…need. I need to be left alone."

Mrs. Van looks at me over my mother's shoulder. "Han-nah! Look! I have made boterkoek. Take it!"

I smile and accept the cake pan from her while Mum glares at me. "Thanks, Mrs. Van."

Mum closes the door. She doesn't say anything to me. I boil the kettle and make myself and Dad a cup of tea.

I carry the tea out to the deck, cut some boterkoek, and bring that too: breakfast. We used to have a cooked family breakfast on Saturday mornings. Katie decided she was vegan and made Mum buy those vegan sausages that look like Plasticine. She sat there with her fake sausages, so self-righteous. Until she tried one. Dad asked her how it was—not even Katie could lie her way out of that one.

My father goes to the tap and turns off the hose. There is a grimace of pain on his face, even though he tries to hide it. He stiffly climbs the steps up to the deck. He has three metal pins in each leg and will never run again. I have never heard him complain about it. Neither he nor Mum ever mentions it. It feels so strange, to watch your own father powerless like that. The person who used to lift us above his head, now chowing down on painkillers, unable to stand for more than an hour.

"Tea?" I ask.

"Cheers, Han." He takes the mug in his hand and lowers himself into the chair. "Your mum want anything?" he asks, even though he knows the answer.

I shake my head. We sip our mugs of tea and look over the gully thrumming in the heat.

"Can I ask about the school counselor?" He waits. "I'm going to take your lack of response as an enthusiastic yes. Is it going OK?"

"It's going OK."

"She any good?"

"She's better than any of the others."

———————

Later that night, I hear them talking. Her voice is not something I know. Neither is his. I should not be here in the hallway. They think I am in bed.

"Are you lying?"

79

"Jeez, Paula. Why don't you just say what's on your mind?"

"If you are lying and you remember what happened and you make her dredge it all up—"

"Why would I do that? If I remembered? Jesus. It wouldn't change anything. The cops are going to go with what she says. Why would I put her through all this if I knew? I'd just tell them. But I'm not going to put my hand up and say, 'Yes, it was all my fault,' if it wasn't. I will go to prison, Paula. And the bastard who was driving the truck, who hit us, he gets off scotfree. Is that what you want?"

"I just want to know what happened."

"So do I. Don't you think I want to know if I killed my own daughter? Do you know what it's like to live with that every day? I want to know. You think I would lie to save my ass?"

Nothing.

"Shit, Paula! Do you even know me? What? Say it!"

"How could you let that happen? She was our baby. You are her father."

"I'll leave. I'll go. I should have gone months ago."

"Where? Where will you go?"

"My brother's, a motel, it doesn't matter."

Silence.

"Do you want me to?"

"It's just…Hannah."

80

"Well, what do you want me to do? I will do it. Whatever you want. If you don't want me here, well, I'll go, Paula. Heck, if you want me to kill myself, I'll do it. It would be a relief."

"Don't you even say that. Don't you even say that. A relief? Why should you get relief from this? Why? Why should you?"

"Do you want me to stay here so you can yell at me?"

And she cries and cries. And then the next day, we all carry on like before.

NINE

Katie's favorite foods:
(Pre-veganism)
* Nanna's lasagna
* Cheesecake
* Peanut M&M's
* Satay anything
* Banana smoothies

(Post-veganism)
* Unsalted cashews
* Organic corn chips
* Satay tofu with vegetables

AT THE VERY edge of Sydney's western suburbs, before the highway climbs into the mountains, there is a large suburb called Penrith. More of a mini-city than a suburb. If there's a rivalry between the upper and lower mountains, it has nothing on the mountains–Penrith feud. We think they're inbred Neanderthals and they think we're inbred snobs. Either way, there's no getting around the fact that Penrith has a mall and the mountains don't. Or the fact that "inbred" is a fairly common insult around here. On Thursday nights, the mall is pretty much just an underage club with swarms of teenagers hanging around, checking each other out. My idea of hell is a PE class held in Penrith's Westfield Mall on a Thursday night.

So you can imagine my delight when the soles of my school shoes finally wear out and I have to go to Westfield to buy a new pair. It used to be the kind of shopping trip Mum would relish. She would drag us from store to store, talking about arch support and heel width. That was before Katie got a job at General Pants and took control of her own school-shoe purchasing.

"I'm pretty sure you're not allowed to wear a two-inch heel to school, Katie."

"Oh yeah, and where are you going in those Clarks, Hannah? The nunnery?"

"At least I don't look like a prostitute. And they're not called nunneries—they're called convents."

"You'd know, you're still gonna be a virgin when you're thirty."

"You'll probably be dead before you're thirty."

———————

Now—as with most things—Mum isn't really interested in school shoes. I'm not really excited about the prospect of a father-daughter shopping trip either—not that Dad would last long walking around. I tell him I'll get the train, and he gives me eighty bucks.

So here I am. Westfield Mall on a Thursday night, Beyoncé ricocheting off the walls, the smell of body spray and McDonald's fries, mums with strollers weaving through hordes of girls in short skirts and guys who pretend they need to shave. And me in my school uniform with eighty bucks in my pocket.

I stand in a shoe shop in front of the school-shoe display—not the kind of store Katie would have gone to. A woman in a polo shirt bounces over to me, her name tag telling the world her name is Trish and there is no foot she can't fit.

"Hiya, sweetie! Just lookin' at school shoes?"

"Um, yeah."

She looks down at my feet.

"Size nine?"

"Yes."

She selects a shoe that looks no different from the others: flat, lace up, black.

"You look like you've got a skinny foot. These are a narrow fit. Good support too." Maybe Mum gives a crap after all and has phoned ahead. "Take a seat over at the fitting station, sweetie, and I'll bring them out."

She gently prods me in the direction of a red vinyl bench seat in the middle of the room. I squeeze between an old woman trying on tennis shoes and a three-year-old using the seat as a gymnastics mat. I sit staring at the opposite wall until Trish reemerges from the stock room. Another salesclerk says something to her and Trish laughs. She kneels in front of me and opens the shoe box.

"You wouldn't believe this woman we had in here before," she says to me, lifting out a shoe wrapped in tissue paper as if it's made of glass. "All dressed up to the nines, wasn't she, Sue?"

The other woman nods. "Gucci handbag and everything. Not a knockoff either, the real deal."

"And she's got this little girl with her, I swear, she had a French manicure. Seven years old! And the woman looks me up and down, and she goes, 'Do you only sell cheap school shoes here?' And I'm like, 'Yeah, no Dior here, dear, you'll have to go somewhere fancy for that.'"

Sue cracks up. Trish smiles and shakes her head. She maneuvers my foot into the shoe and yanks at the laces.

"Talk about more money than sense. We've got damn good school shoes in here. They look good on you, sweetie. Stand up for me. How's the fit?"

She presses her thumb onto the toe of the shoe. Her nails are painted hot pink and have tiny rhinestones set in them. I can imagine my mother's face.

"Enough space there?" she asks.

"Yep."

"How old are you, honey?"

"Fifteen."

"Wow, fifteen. You've still got some growing to do too. Look at the length of her legs, Sue!"

Sue looks at me, her hands on her hips. Tilts her head slightly as she makes her assessment. "Oh, what I'd give to have your height! I bet you'd look gorgeous in a potato sack. And look at all that lovely wavy hair!"

I swallow. There is an ache in the back of my throat and I can't look either of them in the eye.

"Sit back down, sweetie, and we'll put the other one on."

I sit.

Trish kneels down again and laces my other foot into its shoe. "Righto, go for a walk in those."

I walk to the end of the shop, trying to avoid my reflection in the big mirrors.

"Yeah, they're perfect," Trish says. "Have a seat and I'll box them up for you. What school you at?"

"Saint Joseph's, in the mountains."

"Oh yeah, I know the one. My kids catch the train with some of you guys. They're at the middle school. Good school, damn expensive though. My daughter's just like you, you know. Gorgeous-looking girl."

Trish looks up at me with a smile. She pauses. Frowns. "You OK, sweetie?"

Crap. There are tears trickling down my cheeks. I wipe at them with the backs of my hands and nod.

"Oh dear." Sue is there with a box of tissues. She hands me one and I blow my nose. "You had a rough day?"

I nod.

"And some people say the teenage years are the best of your life," Sue says.

"What a load of crap," Trish says. "I'll put these on my account, give you thirty percent off. Go buy yourself a treat."

———

I leave the store under the watchful eyes of Trish and Sue, who tell me there is a sale on at the big department store and it can't be anything some shopping won't fix. I grip the plastic bag my shoes are in and head up the escalator to the bathrooms. The door of the stall slams shut behind me and I crouch down low to the floor.

"Shit, you're ugly."

Cafeteria line. Lunch. Tara curled her glossed lips.

"Maybe she's actually a guy," Amy said. "Are you a guy, Hannah? Do you have a dick?"

I gulp a few deep breaths and slowly stand up again. I put my hand on my stomach and feel the breath moving in and out of my lungs until the static in my head starts to dissolve. All I have to do is get to the station. Get to the station, get on a train, and go home. It isn't far. Breathe in, breathe out, breathe in. I put my head down and leave the bathroom, walking out into the noise of the shopping center. I keep my eyes on the polished floor beneath my feet. There is a tap on my shoulder. It makes me jump with shock. I turn around and there is Josh Chamberlain. He's wearing a hoodie and skinny jeans, even though it's almost ninety outside. His right hand grips a skateboard, its underside decorated with that beautiful

Japanese painting of waves crashing, curls of water like ultra-marine locks of hair. He grins at me like he's in on a joke I don't know about.

"Whoa, what's up with you, Jane Eyre? Look like you're being chased." He looks around. "There a dude in here with a gun or something?"

"Um, no. I don't think so."

He laughs. "What are you doing?"

It takes me a moment to realize he is asking a genuine question, not trying to trip me up. I motion to the bag in my hand. "Shoes. I had to buy school shoes."

"No shit?"

"Ah, no."

"Sweet. I'm just hanging out. Actually, I was supposed to meet this chick, but she hasn't shown. Stood up again, I tell you."

"Sorry to hear that."

"I know. I wore her favorite outfit and everything. Shit. Why did I tell you that?" He shakes his head. "Nah, she's a bitch anyway. She's got no class."

"OK."

We stand there. He looks right at me. His eyes are pale green with little reddish flecks in them.

"I just got off work," he says eventually. "Bowling alley. I'm a dish pig."

I'm not entirely sure what a dish pig is. I don't ask.

"You ever been there?"

Katie used to go there with her fake ID. "No," I answer.

"Yeah, don't think it's your kind of place. I tell you, if you ever do, don't eat the burgers. Just trust me on that one."

"OK."

He grins at me, furrows his eyebrows. "You don't smile a whole lot, do you, Jane Eyre?"

I don't have an answer. I can't figure out why he's still here, talking to me.

"Toughest crowd I've ever had, that's for sure. Where you heading now?"

"Home."

"Ha. Run for the hills."

"Yeah."

"Train?"

"Yeah."

"I'll come with you, make sure you don't get mugged for your school shoes."

"OK."

I walk next to him through the shopping center. The wrist of his left hand is wound with thin strands of leather and braided pieces of string. I wonder if someone made them for him—I can't picture him sitting there patiently braiding away. I can't think of anything to say to him, but he doesn't seem to mind. He doesn't try to make small talk. We weave through the shoppers and out through the automatic doors into the twilight. The heat pushes back at us.

"Friggin' hell," mutters Josh. "There should be a law." He stops walking. "Hold that?" He hands me the skateboard and pulls his hoodie off over his head. There is the musky, fruity scent of his deodorant.

I can feel myself starting to blush, so I turn the board over and study the painting.

"Beautiful, huh?" He hangs his hoodie over his shoulder, starts walking again. "Katsushika Hokusai. *The Great Wave*. Imagine being in the water with that mother comin' at you."

I run my finger over the surface and feel the texture of the brushstrokes. I find my voice. "Did you paint this?"

"Yeah."

"It's really good."

"Hokusai was really good. I'm just good at ripping off other people's shit." He takes the board from me, turns it in his hands. "I'm gonna apply to do an exchange thingy in Japan after junior year. Freaking love Japan. Don't you think the Japanese are the coolest people in the world?"

"Um. I haven't really thought about it."

"If I were Japanese, I would grow my hair really long and get dreadlocks and get this picture tattooed on my arm. Then I'd become a professional samurai warrior."

"Is that an actual occupation?"

"Oh, it would be, Jane. Japan is the coolest place in the world. Did you know that in Japan, they have vending machines for, like, everything? Like clothing and deodorant and everything. So if you're walking down the street and you're like, 'Shit, I forgot to put on deodorant,' you can just go up to a vending machine and buy some."

"Really?"

"Yeah."

"Why couldn't you just go into a store?"

"You don't have time. You're in a hurry—you've got to get to your next samurai gig. See, Japan is all about efficiency. I like that idea. And I just like the idea of buying anything you need from a vending machine."

"Have you been there?"

"Yeah. When I was a kid. Dad had to go there for work, so he took my mum and me and my brother. Pretty much the best two weeks of my life."

We reach the intersection across from the station. I push the button on the pedestrian crossing and wait. He is already halfway across the road, ducking in front of a taxi. It blasts its horn and he gives it a little salute. At the other side, he realizes I'm not there and looks back at me, starts to laugh. I expect him to walk away then. But he doesn't. He waits for the man to turn from red to green. Waits for me to catch up.

"Safety first, huh?" he says. "No, that's the best way, Jane. The Japanese would approve."

We walk to the train platform and he stands next to me until the train arrives. The doors slide open and he gives me a nod.

"Safe travels, Jane."

I can't help but smile. He watches me get on and waits for the doors to close. I take a seat by the window and see him get on his board and skate off toward the exit, gently gliding between commuters.

TEN

Katie's career aspirations (youngest to oldest):

* Unicorn
* Princess
* Movie star
* Catwalk model
* Vet
* Catwalk model
* Olympic swimmer
* Fashion designer
* Stylist

Katie's ultimate dream job:

* Creative director of U.S. <u>Vogue</u> (from what
  I learned reading her questionnaire from her
  career advisor)

SOMEWHERE OVER IN A building, Mrs. Rourke is continuing the noble tradition of torturing students with trigonometry. I, on the other hand, am in Anne's office. She is wearing some sort of muumuu, says it helps her pretend she is on vacation. She has opened all the windows and stands in front of one, fanning her face.

"You'd think with all the money the damn pope has, he could at least buy me an air conditioner."

Mr. Black would probably tell her to pray for one. She sips her mug of tea, plonks herself down opposite me, and takes out her fake cigarette. Katie is there, of course. If I try to picture her at any other time, I can't do it, but here with Anne, she is as clear to me as a photograph.

You gonna talk to her, idiot? Katie asks. She isn't smiling. *You gotta talk to someone.*

"Can you tell me a little about what school was like before Katie died?"

"I thought you said you talked to my dad."

"Yes," she answers slowly.

"Didn't he talk to you about that?" I look at her and she looks back. I want to remind her that she promised not to bullshit me.

"Hannah, I want to hear it from you. They said it was a difficult time for you, that you had trouble fitting in."

I imagine Katie laughing. *That's the understatement of the century.*

"Can you tell me what was happening for you?"

———————

For the first semester of high school, Charlotte and I ate lunch under a big tree with some girls from our old middle school. We weren't really close to the other girls. It was that weird period when everything was so new that you instinctively clung to what and who you knew. I felt that way about the other girls, thought it was different between Charlotte and me. Things stayed that way for pretty much the whole semester, when everything was still exciting and different and I actually believed I might enjoy high school.

It was in the second semester that things began to shift. Charlotte and I both had science at the same time. Our classrooms were right next to each other, and we would meet after and walk down to the big tree for lunch. One day, my science class finished earlier than Charlotte's, so I waited for her outside. She took forever—all the other students came out, but still there was no Charlotte. I looked through the window and saw that she was talking to Tara Metcalf. I waited and then finally they both came out.

Tara gave me the same look as she did on the first day, kind of pitying and disgusted. She flicked her hair and said, "See ya soon" to Charlotte.

Charlotte grinned and gave a nod; then she turned to me. I must have looked pretty disturbed.

"What?" she asked. "Tara's really cool. She's nice when you get to know her."

"I bet." I started walking toward the oval.

Charlotte hesitated. "Wait…"

"What?"

"Tara…um…"

"What?"

"Tara said I should go have lunch with them."

I tried to laugh a bit. "You're not going to, are you?"

Charlotte shrugged and looked away.

"What am I supposed to do?"

"I dunno… Maybe you could come too. I'll ask Tara."

"Gee, thanks. Let me know if you get her permission." I turned and started walking.

"Hannah, wait." Charlotte jogged after me, gave me a friendly push on the arm when she caught up. "I'll come with you," she said.

I pretended nothing had changed for so long.

———

Eventually, the "merger" happened. Charlotte and I moved from our spot under the tree to where the Clones sat at lunch, behind the science wing. It's worth mentioning that Charlotte didn't call Tara and her friends "the Clones." It was the word used by everyone who wasn't one of them. The Clones loved Charlotte. They tolerated me. Charlotte was like the piece of real estate they wanted—I was the crappy old building that they would have to buy as well. And then knock down.

The Clones made it clear I wasn't wanted by acting the complete opposite way. Whenever Charlotte arrived at the ordained lunch spot, they would smile and say hi to her, then look at me with an adapted Tara-dead-animal stare and say, super-perky, "Hi, *Hannah*! You're back! We are so glad. Aren't we?" Cue laughter, at which point Charlotte would pretend not to notice their sarcasm and I would smile and hope that maybe they would miraculously change their opinion of me.

I tried different tactics; I made cookies at home and brought them to school to share around at lunch. None of the Clones would eat one and Tara just looked at me and said, "Um, shouldn't you be cutting back on sugar, Hannah?" Which the rest of the Clones thought was hilarious. And then, after Amy made a comment about my legs being "neon white," I attempted a little DIY fake tanning, which resulted in orange blotches all over my legs, not to mention the palms of my hands. I don't think I need to explain how that went over.

I knew I wasn't wanted. But Charlotte was my oldest, closest friend. I loved her, and I knew that unless I tried to adapt, I would lose our friendship and all the years of history between us. There was also the knowledge that without Charlotte, I would become what is known as a *floater*—someone who doesn't belong, someone without an all-important group membership. An annoying person who keeps popping up and can't be flushed.

When I finally confessed to my mum what was going on at school, she asked me what happened. As if there was one single incident that was to be blamed, as if I'd accidentally stolen Tara's phone or maybe inadvertently told the Clones I thought they were shallow, superficial bitches. Whenever I tried to explain—like telling her that quite often, the lunch spot would be changed and everyone would "forget" to mention it to me or that Tara and Amy would instantly fall silent whenever I happened to show up—she told me I shouldn't let people treat me that way. As if I could turn up and present Tara with the Declaration of Human Rights and point to number seventeen that says "Everyone in the group must be informed of any party, shopping trip, or lunch spot location change." Simple.

And Charlotte. She tried, she really did—she tried to carry

on the illusion we were still the best of bestest friends. She really tried to maintain the facade of loyalty. I was a piece of sentimental childhood memorabilia she couldn't bring herself to throw away.

———————

I clung onto our sinking friendship for the rest of the school year, until the following February, when there was a party at Tara's one Saturday night. Her parents weren't the kind of people to worry about having a hundred kids turn up apparently. And Tara's older brother (one of Katie's friends) reportedly had ten cases of beer in the garage. The whole school seemed to be talking about it; it was all over Facebook. I felt like it was a test, and if I performed well, maybe the Clones would accept me. How pathetic.

Katie was getting a ride with a friend to the party, and I was absolutely not welcome to join her. So it was Dad who drove me. When we were leaving, he asked if I had the invitation so he could punch the address into the GPS. I had to explain that it wasn't the kind of party you got an invitation in the mail for.

"There going to be adults at this party?"

I glanced at him. "I think so. Yes."

"Do you want me to pick up Charlotte? I can give you both a ride. It's no trouble."

"No. She's there already, helping set up."

"I haven't seen Charlotte in ages. How is she doing?"

"OK."

"Met any other cool people at school?"

"Not many."

"Well, Tara must be a good friend if she invited you to her birthday party."

"It's not a birthday party."

"Oh. Still, she's obviously a friend."

We drove on in silence while I redid my hair four times.

Tara's house was at the end of a long street flanked by bush on either side. It was twilight by the time we arrived, and despite the dry summer heat, in the front yard was an upturned oil drum, hungry flames shooting up from the fire within. People gathered around it, laughing in the orange glow. The bodies of two old cars were parked in the long grass. Tara's house was a white-washed weatherboard place. People milled around on the front porch and driveway. I couldn't see Charlotte.

"You sure this is it?" Dad asked.

"Yeah. Um, I think so."

"I might just pop in and say hi to the parents."

"Oh, no, Dad. Really? No, it's fine."

He gave me a look. "Hannah, I'm not going to drive off and leave you here until I've spoken to…someone."

"Maybe I'll just go home. Yeah, let's just go."

"Go? No way! You're not going home. You look beautiful. I'll just say hello to the parents." He got out of the car and headed up the driveway. I felt like I might throw up. Dad waved to the kids on the porch and strode into the house, and I watched them laugh at his back. I wondered whether there was any way I could hide in the front yard somewhere, so I wouldn't be connected with the weird, waving man. He reappeared then with a thin blond woman in a long swishy skirt. I am not exaggerating when I say he pointed at the car and gestured enthusiastically for me to come up to the house. So I did, with the eyes of the growing crowd fixed on me.

"Hannah! This is Tara's mum!"

She was wearing a lot of black eyeliner. She didn't so much smile as assess me with a smirk similar to Tara's signature expression.

"All right," she said and turned and disappeared into the house.

"OK then! See you, Spanner." He gave me a kiss, then jogged down the stairs with a nod to the other kids.

I took a deep breath and headed inside. The house was lit with candles and hanging lanterns. There was the scent of cherry blossom and hair products. The music was beyond loud, and when I caught a glimpse of Tara, she was wearing what appeared to be a black negligee as a dress. She smiled artificially.

"Hi, Hannah! Did your daddy say you could stay?"

I laughed as if she were joking.

It was OK for the first hour or so. I found some of the girls I'd gone to middle school with. I got a seat and a cup of Coke and managed to make my head move in a way that wasn't totally unrelated to the beat of the music. Charlotte even hung with me for a while until she was pulled away by Tom Carey, an older guy who really knew how to wear a T-shirt (and take it off, as it turned out for Charlotte). I saw Katie arrive in a totally different outfit than the one she had left home in: tiny shorts and a white tank top over a silver bikini top. She saw me but ignored me as if we were strangers.

Pizzas arrived, and it was in the kitchen that I bumped into Amy. Literally. She was talking to someone, her back to me. It was crowded, and someone pushed past me, and I bumped into Amy. She spun around, grinning at first, until she saw it was me.

"Oh my God. Hannah McCann totally just grabbed my ass!"

People stopped talking, turned to look. "You little perv! Get off me!"

I stepped back, confused. "Sorry, I didn't mean—"

"Oh my God. Did you guys see that?"

"Yes." Tara's mouth hung open. "I can't believe you groped Amy."

"You can't do that, Hannah! You little lesbo perv. Oh my God." Amy held her hands up, shaking them like she'd touched something gross. Then she rushed out of the kitchen.

"OK," Tara said, giving me her best dead-animal stare. "You totally have to leave. Like, right now."

I looked around to see if someone would come to my defense. Charlotte was there, watching in the doorway.

"Char…" I waited for her to say something in the silence, to rescue me. She said nothing, just stared at me for a few moments and then turned away.

"You need to go, Hannah," said Tara. "Now."

I went out the front door, down the stairs. Katie was standing in the driveway with a group of seniors. She glanced in my direction and, seeing the look on my face and that I was heading toward her, simply raised an eyebrow and mouthed the words *no way*. I gulped and ducked my head as I moved through the people. Katie must have seen me walk away, down the street in the dark. I walked to the end of the street, sat down on the curb, and dialed my dad's number.

———

He was speeding as he came down the street. He pulled the car over next to me and jumped out.

"What happened? Hannah?! Why are you here in the dark by yourself? Where's Katie?"

"I just need you to take me home." The tears came then. I wiped at them, smudging Katie's mascara across my cheeks.

He put both hands on my shoulders and spoke to me softly. "Span, what happened?"

I shook my head. "I just want to go home."

"Did Katie see you like this? Where is she? Why isn't she with you?"

"She's...she's back at the party."

"Did someone hurt you? Did some guy try something?" He looked back up the road, as if for a possible attacker.

"Can we just go?"

"Hop in the car."

I got in and he accelerated down the street to Tara's house. "Dad, no, please."

He pulled up and got out, leaving me in the car. The kids in front of the house looked over and watched him walk up the driveway. Katie narrowed her eyes and gave him the same warning look she'd given me.

"Katie? What's going on? What happened?"

I could see the look of dread on her face. She left the group she was standing with and came over to him, her expression somewhere between mortification and white-hot anger. She said something to him I couldn't hear. Whatever it was, Dad didn't like it.

"Why was your sister down at the end of the street, by herself, crying?" he shouted.

I could see her hissing at him to keep his voice down.

"She was down there, by herself, upset! Why did you let her leave on her own like that?"

"It has nothing to do with me."

He pointed to the car. She stormed down the drive and got in, slamming the door shut. "What the hell, Dad?!"

Dad slammed his own door shut and started the car.

"Dad! This has nothing to do with me!" She glared at me. "Hannah! What the fuck?"

"Watch your language, young lady!"

"Why am I even here? What the hell did I do?"

"What did you do? You let your sister leave that house, in the dark, by herself, when she was clearly upset."

"Why is she my responsibility?"

"She's your sister."

"Yeah and she's a social fucking retard."

"Katherine, you do not speak like that!"

"It's true! This has nothing to do with me." She shifted her death stare in my direction. "Thanks a lot, Hannah. How am I supposed to recover from that? Drag me down too, why don't you."

The next day, I caught the bus to school as usual. I took my normal seat, third from the front on the right. Katie joined her friends in the back. I put my earphones in my ears and watched the road roll past.

Something wet hit my back.

I turned around. There were two Clones sitting in the back near my sister. They were smirking. The rest of the bus shrieked at the brown banana goo seeping through my school shirt. I looked at Katie; she looked back at me, an expression I couldn't read. She didn't say anything.

A message beeped on my phone, private number. "Lesbo Pervert" was all it said. I put it back in my backpack and tried to ignore the rest of the messages that were coming in—my phone was vibrating so much, it almost jumped out of my bag.

I saw Charlotte in the hallway before homeroom. She didn't look at me. She walked straight past. I turned around, followed her, practically ran to catch up to her.

"Charlotte? Where are you going? Charlotte?"

She was trying to stay stoic, but the years of our friendship pulled at her—I could see it in the way she hesitated.

"I can't talk to you."

"Why didn't you do something, Char? You were right there and they were saying that stuff. Why—"

She stopped walking, glanced around nervously. "Did you touch Amy?"

"How could you even think that?"

"It's just a little creepy, Hannah. Why haven't you made any new friends? Why are you so...so into me?"

"Into you? What the hell, Char?"

"You know what I mean." She couldn't look at me. "I feel sick when I think about it, Hannah. I mean, we've slept in the same bed..."

I stood there stunned, tried to put it together in my head.

"I want you to leave me alone, Hannah."

And then she walked away.

———————

Anne's pen doesn't leave the paper as I speak. There is something weirdly validating about having someone write down every word you say as if it is crucially important. When I pause, she looks over what she has written.

"That must have been devastating when Charlotte abandoned you like that. Not to mention your sister."

I don't say anything.

"How do you feel about what happened?"

"Katie never had anything to do with me at school anyway…"

"So you didn't expect her to stick up for you? Hannah?"

I look up at her. "She's dead. I can't…" I let the sentence dissolve. I can't picture Katie in the room anymore. She has gone.

"What about Charlotte?"

I can feel it in my chest, the sharp anger. I focus on the swirly pattern of the carpet.

"Hannah?"

"I don't know. I don't… Can we stop now? Can I go?"

"If you want. But the way you feel about what happened isn't just going to go away if you ignore it."

"I just want to go to class."

She smiles. "Fine. But you promised me no bullshit. Don't forget it."

~~ELEVEN~~

My career aspirations before Katie died:
* Vet
* Author
* Catwalk model (this was the phase when I just
  said whatever Katie said)
* Vet
* Historian
* Anthropologist
* Author

SEVEN THIRTY ON a Sunday morning and I hear a car pull
into the driveway. Without getting out of bed, I peek out my

window and see Nanna striding up the front sidewalk, arms filled with grocery bags. This time, Grandad is trailing behind her. I hear Dad swearing under his breath as he goes down the hall to let them in.

I find my slippers under my bed and pad out into the kitchen. Grandad has parked himself at the table and Dad places a mug of tea in front of him. The steam fogs up his glasses as he takes a sip.

"There she is!" Grandad says when he sees me.

I give him a kiss on the forehead. "What're you guys doing here so early?"

"Don't ask me, love. I'm here under captain's orders." The captain bustles over, dressed all in pastels, gold bracelets shimmering on her pink arms. She gives me a lipstick kiss on the cheek. Dad goes down the hallway, presumably to try to get Mum out of bed.

"Now," Nan says. "Did you pack your golf clubs, Verne?"

"In the trunk," Grandad replies.

"If you leave now, you can get a round in before the heat turns up."

My mother walks down the hallway, hugging her bathrobe around herself. Grandad stands up and goes over to her. He puts his arms around her and she leans her head on his shoulder. He murmurs something to her and she nods.

"I was just saying if the men leave now, they will get a round in before it gets too hot," Nan says.

Nan always refers to Dad and Grandad as "the men." As if they are a subspecies useful for fixing leaking faucets and not much else. Mum doesn't comment on the golf plans. She walks over to the kettle, pours hot water into a mug, and takes it out onto the deck.

Nanna sighs dramatically in a way that is pure Katie. "It's going to be one of those days," she says to Grandad with a glance toward me, as if I'm five years old and don't understand what she's talking about.

"Um, I don't know if Dad will be up for golf, Nan. He can't, um, walk very far."

She raises her drawn-on eyebrows. "Perhaps it will do him good."

Grandad gives me a helpless shrug.

My mother is sitting on the deck. She has perfect posture because my nanna used to make her walk around with a book on her head when she was a girl. Seriously. She is sitting with her back to the screen door, looking out over the gully.

"Hi. Do you want something to eat?" I sound like a waitress. Might as well call her "ma'am."

She turns a little in her chair, looks up at me, her eyes dark and tired. She looks old. "No. Thank you."

"What's Nan doing here?" She has already brought food this week.

My mother sniffs, takes a crumpled tissue from the pocket of her flannel robe. "She thinks we should go through Katie's room. She doesn't think it's healthy to leave it like a shrine."

I look at Mum in her bathrobe, arms wrapped around herself. Withered. She doesn't really look like my mother anymore. I want to go back inside, but I am anchored there, next to her.

"I don't want to get rid of her things," I say.

"I know."

"Do you think we need to get rid of her things?"

She shakes her head, and I don't know if that means she doesn't want to get rid of Katie's things or she doesn't want to talk. I wonder if there's any chance of me sneaking in and getting a few particular items out of Katie's room before they find them. The back door slides open and Nanna sticks her head out.

"Breakfast! Come on, Paula! Hannah!"

———————

The only time I ever eat porridge is when Nanna makes it. She cooks it slowly on the stove, not in the microwave like Dad tries to. She places a steaming bowl down in front of me, dollops a spoonful of honey on top. It doesn't seem right for a summer morning. My mother moves hers around with a spoon.

"I don't know about this," she says.

"It's good for your bowels," Nan replies.

"No, not this. I mean…I don't know if it's a good idea to go through Katie's things today."

Nanna chews a mouthful of porridge, orange lipstick smooshing around on her lips. She swallows. "When are you going to do it then?"

"I think Andrew and I should do it when we're ready."

"Darling, I don't think you should be counting on Andrew." Nanna puts down her spoon and sips her tea. "The fact is, you might well end up on your own."

"I'm not talking about this now."

I put my head down and shovel the porridge into my mouth. It settles in my stomach like wet cement.

"You have to face it, love. I know it's a difficult thing to do, but I don't think you can move forward if—"

"I don't want to move forward."

"Well, that's pretty clear."

Mum shakes her head, jaw tight. Her hand trembles as she moves the spoon around, stirring, stirring.

"Hannah, why don't you go and watch some TV, take your breakfast," Nanna says to me. "Go on, just this once."

I take my breakfast into the living room, keep the volume on the TV down low.

"Have you spoken to the lawyer with him? Do you know what he has said to the lawyer?"

"He was knocked unconscious. He doesn't remember what happened. You know that. I've told you that."

"Is that what he told the lawyer?"

"What? Yes!"

"Were you there when he said it?"

"Mum, for goodness' sake. We are handling it, OK? Leave it."

"Well, from where I'm standing, it all looks like avoidance—avoidance of reality. You can't run from it forever. It's only going to be worse for you if you carry on as if Katherine is about to walk back in the door. The first step you have to take is to go through her things."

Mum doesn't say anything.

"The only way you are going to heal—"

There is a crash—the cracking, exploding sound of porcelain hitting the tiles. I leave my bowl on the coffee table and go to the doorway. Mum stands there, bowl shattered at her feet, porridge splattered everywhere. Nanna makes a move to get up and clean the mess. But my mother speaks, her words hard and forced.

"How can I heal?"

Nanna opens her mouth. Closes it again. Neither of them notice me standing there.

"Go on! You tell me! You tell me what I can do to feel better, you're so full of ideas!"

"Paula—"

"Maybe you can tell Hannah what to do too. Because I haven't just lost one daughter. I've lost both of them."

"No, you haven't." Nanna lowers her voice to a whispery hiss. "But you will if you don't pull yourself together."

"How? Get my hair done? Will that fix it, do you think?"

"It'd be a start. You've got to get back to yourself. Little things make a difference."

"A difference to what? The fact that my daughter was killed and I might be living with the person who killed her?"

Mum sees me then, standing in the doorway. Nanna turns around, begins to say something, but I don't stay to listen. I go down the hall into my room and shut the door. I hear Mum follow me. She knocks on the door, says my name—I don't answer. She knocks again. I pull my desk across the door, blocking it. And then I sit on the floor, underneath the desk, like Katie and I used to do when we were little kids. I sit there for a long time.

Two Facebook pages were created in my honor in the week following the party. The first was "Victim's of Hannah McCann Unite!" (The Clones didn't have the best grasp of punctuation.) It said I was a lesbian sexual predator. Two days later, there was another: "Hannah McCann is a Man!" The fact that I couldn't be a man and a lesbian didn't bother them. Added to that were the unflattering pictures of me the Clones put on their Instagram accounts when they weren't posting selfies.

Katie didn't speak to me until Friday afternoon when we were walking home from the bus stop.

"So? What are you going to do to fix the fact that you're the resident freak?"

I must have looked surprised.

"Just so we're clear: I'm only talking to you because I feel sorry for you. I am still pissed off at you for dragging me into your fucking mess."

"I didn't drag you into anything."

"So what was Dad's little display at Tara's party about?"

"I didn't blame anything on you."

"I noticed you didn't stand up for me either."

"I didn't stand up for you?! Are you serious?"

"You're not exactly drowning in friends at the moment, Hannah. So I wouldn't be playing the blame game if I were you."

TWELVE

Katie's most played songs:
* "Cannonball"—The Breeders
* "Lithium"—Nirvana
* "Arabella"—Arctic Monkeys
* "Gold Lion"—Yeah Yeah Yeahs
* "Pictures of You"—The Cure
* "New York, I Love You"—LCD Soundsystem
* "Heavy Soul"—The Black Keys
* "Lust for Life"—Iggy Pop
* "London Calling"—The Clash
* Basically every song from the Trainspotting soundtrack
* "While My Guitar Gently Weeps"—The Beatles

THE FOLLOWING NIGHT, when my parents are asleep, I get up and go into Katie's room. I turn on her bedside lamp and close the door behind me. I pull back her comforter and lie down on her bed. She would be pissed off about me invading her space, I'm sure. But she is gone, completely and utterly not here. The sheets haven't been changed since the last time she slept in them—Mum wouldn't let Nanna in here, and I think Nanna was too scared of her smashing more stuff if she pushed her. On the floor under Katie's bedside table is her laptop in its case. I lean over and pick it up. I prop her cushions up behind me and set the computer on my lap. I plug the power cord into the outlet by the table. The top of the case has a fine layer of dust on it. I open it and push the power button. It takes a few moments before the screen lights up and the laptop plays three chords, announcing its return to consciousness.

I open her browser, click on the history tab, and unfurl the list of websites she last visited. There are several fashion blogs, Facebook, Twitter, more fashion blogs, and several university sites. I follow the links and find a course outline for a bachelor of arts in communications (information and media) and another for a course in fashion journalism at a design school. The grades needed to get in are really high. There is another link to information about the swim program at the Australian Institute of Sport. I close the browser and go into her media file.

She would scream at me if she could. I open her photo folder and thousands of shots of Katie and her friends splash across the screen. I scroll through them. There are none of me and her, none of her and Jensen. Jensen's face doesn't appear anywhere.

I knocked on her bedroom door and waited. Waited, waited. Finally, it opened a fraction, and she stood there without saying anything like, "Come on in!" or, "Yeah, I'd love to have a sisterly chat and hear all about your problems."

"Permission to enter?" I asked.

She contemplated me for a moment, and I wondered if she was going to ask me to fill out a visa application. Then she opened the door farther and stepped aside. She closed the door behind me. Her bed was covered with textbooks and torn notebook pages scrawled with handwriting. I went to move some aside, make some room, but she beat me there, sweeping them into a pile, her face ducked away from mine. Almost like she was embarrassed. That would be a first.

"I'm sort of busy. What do you want?"

I sat on her bed.

She rolled her eyes and sat next to me.

"I just… I just want to…talk. I don't know what to do. You've never had to deal with…this…and I—"

She gave a short laugh, scoffing.

"What? You haven't."

"Well, that's bullshit."

"What? When?"

"No, no, go on. I'm all ears," she said in a way that suggested the opposite.

"I just… You have to tell me what to do, Katie."

She took a deep breath, turned to face me. "OK. Let's talk about this. Are you, in fact, a lesbian? And before you answer, there is nothing wrong with being a bit lez, OK? So. Are you?"

"No! Katie, I'm not gay!"

"OK, you need to calm down then because, like, the lady doth protest too much or whatever."

"Since when do you quote Shakespeare?"

"Let's get this straight. Ha, sorry—"

"That's not even funny."

"Yeah, it is. Did you or did you not give Amy whatsherface a bit of a, you know, bit of a feel up?"

"Katie! I just told you."

"OK. So no girlie love going on then. I mean, of all people, I'd be surprised if you went for her."

"Just tell me what I should do."

"You mean aside from publicly making out with some guy?"

"Preferably."

She pulled her hair forward over her shoulder, twisted it around and around. "Because that would help."

"Katie. Come on."

"Although, then they'll just call you a slut, so it's lose-lose."

"Thanks."

"Spanner, I don't know. You care too much. You care too much what people think of you. It's obvious, and it makes it easy for them, you know?"

"I make it too obvious that I don't like having food thrown at me?"

"You just…" She sighed. "You just want them to like you so much. You need to stop trying so hard."

"Stop trying not to get called a lesbian? It's easy for you to say all this when everyone thinks you're a goddess."

She released her hair and it fell loose, untwisting. "Yeah? And where's that going to get me exactly, Hannah? Jeez, you're naive. Leave it. Just leave it. Stop taking everything so seriously. They'll get bored. They'll move on. Can you go now? I'm busy. I've got an English essay."

"Yeah? What on? Gatsby?"

"Seriously, Hannah, leave. Now."

"I can, you know, look at it if you want."

"Out."

I sit at the agriculture plot during lunchtime with my legs stretched out in the sun, back against the shed's wall, and listen to Katie's iPod. I am up to number 159: "Heart-Shaped Box" by Nirvana.

Up until the last few days, I knew very little about Nirvana other than the fact that Kurt Cobain shot himself in the head. After listening to "Lithium," "Drain You," "Come as You Are," "Jesus Doesn't Want Me for a Sunbeam," and now "Heart-Shaped Box," I feel I know Kurt Cobain quite well.

The goats pick their way through the long grass, chewing their feed with little corn teeth, bleating occasionally. Then suddenly, they startle, heads bobbing up, before turning and skittering down the far side of the paddock. I look around, tug my earphones from my ears. If a teacher finds me, it will be interesting to see if they give me a detention for being out of bounds. But it's not a teacher. It's Josh Chamberlain.

He dumps his backpack a few yards from me, leans against the wall like he is waiting for a bus.

"Hey," he says, super casual.

"Hey." I wait. He doesn't say anything more but takes a small folded piece of paper and a pen from his pocket. He unfolds the paper and squints at it.

"Noxious weed. Seven letters, fourth letter *t*?"

124

"I beg your pardon?"

"Noxious weed. Seven letters, fourth letter *t*. Oh, wait. Last letter *a*."

"Lantana?"

"Bingo. Well done, Jane. Animal dance, seven letters, third letter *x*?"

"That's easy: fox-trot."

"Easy for some, Jane."

"Are you doing a crossword puzzle?"

"No. I'm just asking you random questions. Yes, I'm doing a crossword. What are you doing around here?"

"Just having lunch."

"In secret. Very mysterious. Chicken, seven letters? Wait. Poultry." He writes on the piece of paper. "Nice shoes by the way."

"Excuse me?"

"Your shoes. They're new, right?"

"Oh yeah."

"You're gonna get busted if you're caught down here, 'specially with me."

"I was here first."

"You'll have to speak up. I can't hear a word you're saying."

I swallow. "I was here first," I repeat, a little louder.

He gives me a grin. "Whoa, did you just crack a joke, Jane? I'm pretty sure you did. Stop the presses."

I feel myself blushing, feel my breath drain from my lungs. The feeling that this is all a nasty prank resurfaces. But Josh is still smiling.

"My mate got expelled for being out of bounds," he says. "Can you believe that? Who gets expelled for being out of bounds? He used to go down by the lake and sell his dad's smokes to kids from here."

Probably to my sister.

"School couldn't prove it though, so they just punished him for being out of bounds. He works up on the Gold Coast now. Movie World. Wears a Bugs Bunny suit or something. Don't laugh. I'm dead serious. Says he's gonna get me a job working the Batman ride. You ever been on the Batman ride?"

"Um. No."

"You should. It's a very good ride. Very clever stuff. Helps if you like Batman though. I like Batman, but I can't watch the second one—the one with Heath Ledger. Man, that freaks me out. Does my head in."

Josh slides his back down the wall and sits next to me. He takes two cigarettes from his pocket, holds one out to me. "Care to join?"

"Um, no thank you."

"Wise choice." He puts a cigarette between his lips. The

other he sticks behind his ear. "Cigarettes will kill you, Jane. So how come you're around here all on your lonesome?"

"It's complicated."

"Smoking a joint, I bet. I tell you, it's always the quiet ones. Why are you smiling? Drugs are no joke, Jane."

He lights the cigarette, inhales, and breaks into a coughing fit, which seems strange for someone who's used to smoking. "I'm new here, in case you hadn't noticed. And I don't think you have noticed, 'cause I've tried to get your attention several times and you've just…" He moves his flat palm up and down in front of his face, expressionless.

"Stonewalled me. Straight up. Have you considered taking up professional poker playing? 'Cause I think you've got a real skill there."

"But, um, I talked to you in Penrith…"

"Yes you did. But the other day, I was in the library writing some poetry and you walked in and I'm all, like, waving and shit and you didn't even see me."

"Really?"

"Yes, really."

"I'm sorry."

"Apology accepted."

"You came from Reacher Street High, didn't you?"

"Yep! Hallelujah, I've been saved by the Catholic school

system! My mum's got this effed up idea that I should go to a Catholic school for the Higher School Certificate. Makes Dad pay the school fees. Part of the divorce settlement. She would have gone private, really stuck it to him, but not even good ole Dad could afford that. Totally sucks though, if you ask me—he has to pay for a school I don't even want to go to. She's just doing it to piss him off. Your parents divorced?"

"Not yet."

He stubs out the half-smoked cigarette and throws it into the paddock. Which also seems odd for someone who smokes.

"You can't do that," I say.

"Pardon?"

"Throw your cigarette away like that. You'll start a fire."

He laughs. "I don't see a fire."

"That's how they start."

"Who are you? Officer Sensible?" Josh gets to his feet, jumps down off the porch onto the grass. He ducks down, picks up the cigarette, and holds it up for me to see. "Phew! Disaster averted." He hoists himself back onto the porch. It's not much of an effort—he's very tall. "Well?" he asks, sitting back down.

"What?"

"Aren't you going to thank me?"

"For picking up a cigarette that you threw on the ground in the first place?"

"I notice you don't have a bunch of friends. Wonder why that is?"

I don't say anything.

He holds up his palms in surrender. "Sorry, sorry, I know, I know. I'm supposed to be nice to you."

"What?"

He shrugs.

"What?"

"You know." He stops, bites his lip. "Your sister. I remember that morning, a year ago, yeah?"

Everyone remembers that morning. People around here are still talking about the traffic delays it caused.

"Yes."

"Were you in the car too?"

"Yes."

"What happened?"

"A truck hit the car."

"Shit."

"Yeah."

We sit in silence for a while. Josh takes a bottle of Coke from his backpack. Has a swig. "Do you miss her? Sorry, that's a really dumb question."

I think of all the people who have asked me that: people with framed diplomas on their walls and couches in their offices.

"We didn't get along very well. But yes."

The goats have slowly made their way back up the paddock. They watch us warily, chewing the grass.

"So why are you around here by yourself?"

"Like you said, I'm no good at the whole friendship thing."

"I like how you say that as if having friends is a fad you don't think will catch on."

"That pretty much sums me up."

"Ah, Jane. You're not so bad. Just need to work on your attitude a bit."

"Oh?"

"Yeah. I've done a lot of work on my attitude under Black's recommendation. Was headed for a life of crime, you see, before kind Mr. Black swooped in and saved me from myself. He'd be concerned about you if he knew you were out of bounds. It's a slippery slope. That's what he told me. One minute, you're drinking your soda behind the agriculture building. Next, you're robbing a bank. You're laughing again, Jane. You gotta take this seriously. Not a joke."

The bell rings for class.

Josh picks up his backpack. "What's next for you?"

"Biology."

"Same. Hey, let's just stay here, could have a little biology lesson of our own." He grins.

I fail to hide my shock.

"That was a joke, Jane. See, you were doing well—you got the others—but you missed that one. Can I walk with you? Or do I need to marry you first?"

"You can walk with me. But no more jokes."

"Wouldn't dream of it."

THIRTEEN

"What do you think Katie thought of you?" Anne asks me.

"I don't know."

"Really? You seem like a fairly emotionally intelligent person, Hannah. Take a stab."

Yeah, Hannah, says Katie. *Take a stab. Take a stab at me.*

"Because do you know what it looks like from my side?" Anne asks.

I shake my head.

"It looks like it isn't the accident you don't want to talk about. It's Katie."

"Maybe."

"I'm not letting you off the hook. What do you think Katie thought of you?"

"She was disappointed in me."

"How?"

"She said I needed to grow a spine."

"With regard to the bullying?"

"With regard to everything."

"You're a gentle person, aren't you, Hannah?"

I shrug because I've never heard it described like that. "And it sounds to me like there were elements of Katie that weren't gentle."

Here we go, says Katie. *Let's psychoanalyze the dead girl so we can hang all the shit on her, 'cause she's not gonna know, right?*

"I wonder if maybe she saw something of herself in you sometimes and she didn't like it," Anne says. "Maybe she saw you as vulnerable, and vulnerability wasn't something she was comfortable with, especially in herself, so she tried to stamp it out. Maybe in a strange way, she was trying to protect you."

———————

The beach house wasn't all it was cracked up to be—namely due to the glaring lack of beach. My mother had stood on the back deck examining the view of trees and rooftops, her purse still over her shoulder even though we'd been there half an hour. She was reluctant to commit, I guess.

"It said 'water views,'" she said. "I double-checked, triple-checked."

Dad gently slipped the bag strap from her shoulder. "Well, I mean, it's still a nice view. Lots of trees," he said.

"We have a better view at home."

Dad walked the length of the deck, craned his neck sideways. "There! I see it! The ocean! Through those trees, just next to that apartment building. Do you think it's an apartment building? Could be offices, I suppose. Council offices maybe."

Mum stood in front of him, and he steered her shoulders in the right direction.

"Do you see it? Do you?"

"I see it." She took her bag from him and went inside.

"Katie," Dad called. "I found the view! Come see."

"You found the view?" Already in her bikini, Katie padded across the timber decking. "Doesn't inspire confidence, Dad."

"Look." He pointed.

Katie laughed. "Well, at least they made up for it with these very tasteful dolphin wind chimes. And so many. Just in case we forget we're at the beach."

"Do not say that to your mother."

It turned out the phrase "walking distance to beach" was also largely relative. It was walking distance to the beach in comparison to our house, for example. The walk looked as if it would take about twenty-five minutes, so when you finally made it home after a refreshing swim, you'd need another one to cool off again.

"It's not a problem," Dad said. "We'll just go to the beach as a family. That's the point of a vacation."

Katie didn't make an effort to hide her objection to nothing-but-all-family beach time. It's hard to flirt with lifeguards when your dad is right there in a pair of baggy trunks.

So it was agreed that Katie and I would walk to the beach in the mornings. Mum and Dad would come and meet us in the afternoons for the quality family time Dad was so eager to have.

On the first morning, Katie emerged from her bedroom wearing her chosen beach attire: a pearlescent white bikini, which was basically just a collection of strategically placed triangles.

"Interesting," my mother said. "And what are you going to cover up with?"

"I have a towel," Katie replied, as if Mum were a little on the slow side.

"Maybe a T-shirt and skirt would go nicely with the towel?" Mum suggested.

I, on the other hand, had the art of covering up down pat.

A long tankini top and trusty board shorts that almost reached my knees. There was zero chance of my attire becoming dislodged by a rogue wave.

"What are you wearing?" was Katie's response to my ensemble.

"It's a tankini."

"Yeah, see, 'tankini' is another word for middle-aged, I'm-a-little-dumpy-now swimsuit. Seriously, Hannah? Where did you get that? And are those men's shorts? Oh my God. I'm not going to the beach with you looking like that."

"Katherine," Mum said. "Leave her alone."

"I will. That is exactly what I will do."

"You're only going if you go together."

Katie took my wrist and dragged me into her room. "Do you seriously have nothing else you can wear?"

"Um. I have my racerback."

"This isn't swim practice, Hannah."

"I'm not comfortable just in, you know…" I motion to her *Sports Illustrated* ensemble.

"Why? You don't wear frigging board shorts at practice. Oh. But you do cover your butt with your kickboard when you're walking over to the pool, don't you? Yeah, I've seen you doing that—not exactly subtle."

She began to rummage through her suitcase. "It's lucky I have five bikinis."

She tossed one in my direction. Blue polka dots.

"Just put it on, Hannah. It's cute. You're cute. We'll be cute together."

Katie chose a spot on the sand, spread out her towel, and lay down on her stomach. (On top of the towel rather than under it as Mum might have hoped.) I kept mine wrapped around me like a thermal double-layer tube dress with extra padding—just what every girl needs on the beach.

"Are you just gonna sit there like that?"

"Yes."

"That's a really big hat by the way."

"Well, it's a really big sun. And it's eating your skin while we speak."

"I'd rather take my chances with the sun than cover myself with carcinogenic chemicals."

"Convenient argument for someone so fond of tanning."

"I'll make you give me my swimsuit back. Now."

And then…five, four, three, two, one.

"Have I seen you here before?" Wet suit rolled down to the waist, board under the arm, sun-bleached hair. Big smile. They were always so friendly. And inventive with their opening lines.

"Oh, hey." She sat up, shielded her eyes from the sun with

one hand and removed her sunglasses with the other. She wasn't a *Sports Illustrated* model. She was Elizabeth Taylor.

"Maybe. How's the swell?" Did she research this stuff beforehand? Get the right lingo?

"Crowded. Choppy too."

He dropped the board and sat on the sand.

"I'm Campbell." (Like the soup.)

He offered his hand; she shook it.

"Kate."

He turned to me.

I shook his hand. "H-Hannah."

"And here's the dickhead who kept running into me." Another one now. Darker. Tattoo climbing his calf. He dropped his board and reached behind his back to unzip his wet suit.

"Ya had no chance, Campbo." He peeled the wet suit from his shoulders, pulled each arm free. If these guys were our age, they were taking an awful lot of steroids. "Who're your friends?"

"Hannah and Kate."

"Heath. How's it goin'?"

"Good," replied Katie.

"You aren't from here, are you?" He grinned.

Katie laughed. Not too much. She measured it perfectly. "Yeah, we're on vacation."

"Sisters?"

"Uh-huh. Cold in there?"

"Oh no. Campbo, whada ya think? Seventy-seven, seventy-eight degrees?"

"Seventy-eight for sure. You gotta get in there."

"Hmm. Yeah right." She stood up, adjusted a strategically placed triangle. "Let me guess, there're dolphins too, right?"

"Lots of them." Campbell got to his feet. The expression "kid in a candy store" wouldn't be too far off.

"Watch our stuff, Han?" Katie tossed her sunglasses to me.

"No way," Heath said, and it occurred to me he was looking at me. "You're going in too." He held out his hand to help me up. (I obviously needed it, what with my beach-towel cocoon and all.)

"No, no. I'll just stay here."

"Na-ah. Can you swim?"

"She can swim." Katie fixed me in her gaze, raised an eyebrow, seeing if I would accept the challenge.

I took his hand and allowed myself to be pulled up while keeping a firm grip on the towel. Maybe I could shout "Look over there!" and run into the water while they were distracted. Very sophisticated.

Campbell and Katie were already heading to the water. Heath was waiting for me. This was definitely the closest I had ever been to a half-naked male. I swallowed. Removed my hat. And unwrapped the towel. Just my fluorescent skin and a few polka dots. Excellent. He grabbed my hand and pulled me toward the water.

Later, Heath asked a lot of questions. What was surprising was that he addressed them to me. He also offered to put sunscreen on my back. I responded by opening my mouth in an effort to speak. And failing. When I think back to that day on the beach, I can barely believe I was even there. It feels like the chunk of a film that never made the final cut. Arrangements were made. They would be back at the beach at six thirty, would pick us up; we would go have drinks.

Katie told Mum and Dad that the two of us were going to walk into the town to catch a movie (not about to engage in some kind of drug-fueled orgy, as *Cosmo* would have them believe). If they were suspicious about the amount of preparation time that we put in, they didn't let on. I was, after all, the perfect accomplice for Katie.

The dress was blood orange. Strapless. Tiny blue buttons in the shape of sparrows ran down the front of the bodice to the waist. It wasn't mine, of course. She said the color went with my dark hair. Complemented.

We stood in the tiny strip of space between the two single

beds. Starfish-patterned curtains drawn, a pastel painting of a little girl with a basket of seashells looking us over. Katie was twisting her curls into a side knot below her left ear. She took a bobby pin from the selection she held between her lips and pushed it into the coil of hair.

"You want earrings?" she asked.

"I don't have pierced ears, remember?"

She took the last bobby pins from her mouth and slid them into her hair. "Holy shit, Hannah. What century do you live in? It's not illegal, you know. You have shaved your legs, haven't you? Show me. You did behind the knees, right? Oh God, Hannah. Here's a razor—can you hurry?"

"Is he really going to be looking at the back of my knees?"

"He's a guy. He's going to be looking everywhere. You look pale. Are you going to pass out? You need to look at this as an opportunity, OK? This is experience. You need experience. You might even enjoy yourself."

She sounded like our mother.

———————

The twilight air crawled over my bare shoulders. We walked the edge of the road, sandals scattering the gravel. The girl who was playing me was trying to look confident.

"How old are they, Katie?"

"You don't want to be with guys your age. Trust me. We mature earlier anyway. Heath's gorgeous. Like it matters how old he is."

"Is he driving? Do you think that's because he's older?"

She gave me a sideways glance. "Are you backing out on me? I can't go unless you do. You know that. You look pretty. It'll be fun."

"What about Jensen?"

"Fuck, Hannah. We're not going to marry these guys. Look." She stopped walking, stood in front of me. "This is practice. You have to take every opportunity you can to get practice. These guys are a rehearsal. Someone like Jensen…" She sighed. "Jensen is… He's a whole other level. If I get it wrong with Jensen, I'm not going to get another chance. This is as close as I get to sisterly advice, Span. Take it. Experience is everything."

You could feel the air thickening with salt as we neared the beach. The grumble and sigh of waves pounding soft sand. I felt as though my heart and lungs had decided to quit and left me. Given up already. The girl who was playing me was losing her place. And then she turned and then she was running. There was someone calling after her. But she didn't stop.

Furious doesn't quite cover it. She was so pissed off, she didn't talk to me until the next day—the beach again, no sign of Heath and Campbell.

"I do not understand you. What the hell was that about? Shit. No wonder, Hannah. No wonder you get so much crap at school."

"I'm sorry."

"I thought you liked them. Seriously, what's not to like? Are you gay?"

"No."

"Then what?"

"I don't know. I just… I just freaked out."

"Yeah, you did. What? You think you were going to get raped or something?"

"I don't know."

"Why do you have to take everything so fucking seriously?"

"I just didn't want to have to…"

"To what?"

"I'm not you."

"You're not me? What the fuck does that mean, Hannah? You mean you're not a slut, like me? That what you mean?"

"I didn't say that." I was crying. Sitting on the beach in a polka-dot bikini crying.

"Don't you dare judge me. What? So if you're the smart one,

does that make me the bimbo slut? Does it? You think I'm so stupid that all that's left for me is to screw around?"

"No. Katie, I don't think that. Please. I'm sorry about last night. I was… I don't know."

"You ask me what you should do. You're always like, 'Katie, how do I get them to stop picking on me?' Well, I don't know, Hannah, maybe stop acting like you've got such a big stick up your ass. You are so unbelievably stuck up."

"I'm not stuck up. How does being scared make me stuck up?"

"What are you scared of? Why do you have to take everything so fucking seriously?"

———————

I am in my room when the taxi pulls into the driveway. I can see it from the desk by my bedroom window. The passenger-side door swings open. My father. One leg and then the other. Hands brace, one on the door, the other on the roof of the car. He slams the door shut behind him, limps down the sidewalk to the mailbox. He takes from it one single letter, stands gazing at it in his hand. In the kitchen, I hear my mother turn on the radio and turn it off again. She opens and closes cupboards, a faucet runs. My father stands there looking at the letter in his hands, turns it over, and I can see that it's a postcard, not a letter. We don't know anyone who might be in the kind of place you send a postcard from. A place where we are missed. He puts the postcard in his pocket.

After dinner, I take our plates into the kitchen and open the dishwasher. I hold the first plate, my mother's—laden with uneaten food—and push the pedal on the trash can with my foot. On top of a mound of potato peels is a postcard—or rather, two halves of a postcard. I set the plate down on the bench and extract both pieces, hold them together. The picture is of snow-capped mountains and a blue sky. Greetings from Zurich!

Dear Katie and Hannah,

How are you both? I am good. The conference is going well. I've met some amazing people. Zurich is a really nice place, lots of good chocolate! Next time, I will bring you guys and your mum along. Look after her for me. I miss you.

Lots of love,
Dad

He was overseas about a month before the accident. He'd written down the wrong zip code. The postcard has been floating in the great land of undelivered mail all this time. Finally found its way home, a year too late.

I take the postcard into my room and stick it together with Scotch tape. Then I go into Katie's room, open her desk drawer, and put the postcard inside.

~~FOURTEEN~~

Life advice Katie gave me:

* Ignore the health warnings; smoking is hot.
* If you see something in a store but it's too expensive, take a red pen, cross out the price, and write next to it what you want to pay. The salesclerk will think it's on sale. (Don't make it too low though. They get suspicious.)
* Breakfast is the easiest meal of the day to cut out.
* Don't drink mixed drinks. It's the sugar in them that makes you feel worse the next day. They also make you fat.

JOSH IS IN my math class. He sits opposite me with two other Reacher Street High kids. The desks are arranged in a horseshoe shape, probably to encourage dynamic class discussions or something. Mrs. Rourke, my math teacher, clearly despises the arrangement. She doesn't really encourage any interaction between students. She also doesn't respond well to questions. You get the feeling she'd prefer it if there were no actual students there so she could get through the lesson without interruption.

Katie would say it's stuck up to say this, but none of the other kids in the class are what you would call especially "academic." It's the second-lowest math class. Pretty much everyone else here is in detention at least once a week for various violations of school rules. Then there's me. I'm just crap with numbers. Most of my other classes, I get A's. Mrs. Rourke has sensed that I hate math—or maybe less sensed and more noticed from my endlessly incorrect answers. She doesn't offer any smiling encouragement but instead treats me like a disease she can't cure.

Today, she writes a series of algebra problems on the whiteboard. She begins to explain—for about the five hundredth time—how to find x. Josh, of course, puts his hand up.

"Yes?"

"I found x, ma'am. It's up at the top there, next to the six."

She lets out a long breath. "Do I have to ask you to leave, Mr. Chamberlain?"

"Ma'am, I'm just trying to help out."

"Shut up and listen."

"Yes, ma'am."

She continues with her droning, monotone explanation. It takes me a moment to realize that Josh is staring directly at me. I look over to him and he crosses his eyes. I look away, but when I glance back, he is still doing it: sitting there looking directly at me with his eyes crossed. As directly as it is possible to look with your eyes crossed, I suppose. Mrs. Rourke notices him. Her eyes dart from Josh to me. She is confused. Post Katie, I am off-limits to any kind of harassment by other students. Everyone knows it. But it is clearly inconceivable that anyone would be socializing, no matter how subliminally, with me. She ignores the incident like she is sure she is seeing things and moves on to the next problem. I glance at Josh; he crosses his eyes again.

Mrs. Rourke folds her arms.

"Mr. Chamberlain, do you have a problem?"

"Yeah, ma'am. Thanks for asking. I have a lot of problems and I just don't know where to turn anymore."

She purses her lips and narrows her eyes. "One more interruption and you can leave."

He gives her a salute. Mrs. Rourke uncaps her marker and carries on talking about x and y. She turns and writes on the whiteboard, and as her back is turned, Josh tosses a ball of paper at me. It's a situation I have been in so many times before: kids harassing me while the teacher isn't looking. It practically used to be a school sport—let's see how much shit we can give Hannah without the teacher noticing. But now the rules are different. Mrs. Rourke turns to us and starts talking again. Josh watches her with a straight face. She turns back to the board. Josh looks pointedly at the ball of paper on my desk. *I dare you*, he mouths.

The other students, including Tara and Amy, are watching. They've never seen the game played like this before. Tara looks completely confused. I pick up the ball and throw it just as Mrs. Rourke turns around to face us. Her mouth drops open in shock.

"Miss McCann, I would expect better from you." She points to Josh first, then me. "Both of you, out."

I have never been kicked out of class before. I don't quite know what to do. Leaving would be a good start.

Josh stands up.

Mrs. Rourke glares at me. "Hannah?"

Do I pack up my stuff and take it? Do I leave it? Josh has left his and is heading out the door, so I do the same and follow him. Outside, he stands with his hands in his pockets and a wicked grin on his face. He shakes his head. "Jane, Jane, Jane. I'm trying to better my mathematical skills. Stop dragging me down. Ha, look at your face. It's OK. You're not going to get expelled."

Mrs. Rourke opens the door and steps out. She looks at us both, her jaw tight.

"Mr. Chamberlain, what do you have to say for yourself?"

"Ma'am! She was the one throwing stuff." He winks at me.

"Miss McCann?"

"Um. I'm…um, sorry."

"Your grades would hardly suggest you are in a position to be messing around in class."

"Yes."

"Consider yourselves warned. Another word from either of you and you can go to the principal's office."

"Message received, ma'am," Josh says.

"Get back to your desks."

When I get home from school, Mrs. Van is in her front yard, pulling at the cord of her lawnmower. It ignores her. She wipes her forehead with her arm. She wears baggy pajama shorts, socks with sandals, and her Big Banana T-shirt. It's her favorite T-shirt—I know that because she told me once. Her son bought it for her; he lives in Coffs Harbor. I've never seen him.

"Look at my lawn!" she says when she sees me. "So overgrown."

It looks like a putting green.

"It won't start," she says in a way that implies the lawnmower is lazy rather than broken.

"Do you want me to try?"

"Oh, you are such a good girl."

I dump my backpack on the sidewalk and go over to the lawnmower. I give the starter cord a good tug and the mower grumbles to life. Mrs. Van claps; she motions to take the mower from me. I shake my head.

"You shouldn't be doing this," I say. I push the mower along next to the fence. It doesn't take long to do the lawn. The grass smells good, like childhood. It reminds me of summer vacation when Dad would put the sprinkler on the lawn and Katie and I would run around in our swimsuits. When I am finished, I glance up and see my mother watching me from our kitchen window. I smile, but the sun is reflecting off the windowpane and I can't see her expression.

"I don't see your mother leave the house," Mrs. Van says.

"She doesn't go out much at the moment."

"It is very bad for her to be inside all day. Very bad for the head not to see the sunlight."

I pick up my backpack. "Well, see you, Mrs. Van."

"It has been almost a year since Katie was killed."

She doesn't say "passed away" like everyone else. I despise the term "passed away." It sounds peaceful and graceful and kind of magical. I don't think there was anything peaceful about Katie's death.

"That is a long time to stay in the house."

"Yeah. It is."

"But there is nothing like the pain of burying your child. It is the worst kind of agony." She closes her eyes for a moment. Then opens them and puts a hand on my arm. "I am very tired. Too old! I will go inside. You go to your mother."

In the evening, Mum sits at the dining table, sorting through a pile of paperwork from the lawyers. The fan whirs around back and forth, snatching papers and tossing them to the floor. Rather than move the fan or turn it off, Mum just repeatedly picks the papers back up, swearing under her breath.

I have ventured from my room because it is stifling in there, no breeze at all through the window. Plus, it is dinnertime supposedly. Although my mother seems oblivious.

"Um, are you going to eat anything?"

She looks up from the table, frowning as if I have said something deeply offensive. "What, Hannah?"

"It's just, I thought I might get something to eat."

"Fine." She turns back to her work.

"Shouldn't Dad be home by now? It's after seven."

She dismisses the question with a wave of her hand. "I don't know. Maybe he has a meeting."

"OK. I might make some spaghetti. Dad will probably want dinner when he gets home."

"Yes," she sighs. "Dad will probably want dinner."

"Or maybe I'll just do some instant noodles. It might be too hot to cook spaghetti."

She isn't listening.

I take a box of two-minute noodles from the cupboard, split it open, and drop the square of dehydrated curls into a bowl. I shake the loose noodles out—like the tiny bones of a delicate creature—and scatter the powdered flavoring over the top. Through the kitchen window, I see a taxi approach our driveway and stop. The passenger-side door opens and my father begins to slowly extract himself, puppet-like, from the car.

The taxi driver gets out, walks behind the car, and opens the trunk. He pulls out Dad's crutch, hands it to him, and puts his briefcase and laptop bag on the grass.

The taxi drives off, leaving my dad standing alone with two bags he can't carry.

I go outside, and he smiles but doesn't meet my eyes. I pick up the bags, and he follows me, limping, up the sidewalk to the house.

"Hi, Hannah!"

They slid into the seat behind me, Tara and Amy. Always the Tara and Amy show. The bus swayed as students climbed on. I couldn't see Katie out the window. She was usually right at the back of the line, no rush—practically had a bus seat reserved in her name.

"How was your day, Hannah?" Amy asked. "Get any lesbian action in the library? Or were you at it all by yourself?"

I kept my focus on the window. Katie had advised me to stick to the "ignore them and they'll go away" strategy. This was highly doubtful. In the Canadian Rockies, for example, cougars are known to stalk unsuspecting campers for up to three days before they strike—no matter how good their prey are at ignoring them.

"Han-nah, you're being so rude!" Tara said. "Amy's just trying to make conversation. Aren't you into Amy anymore? Just into yourself?"

Amy laughed as if she were in front of a camera. Students continued to file onto the bus, but the flow was slowing to a trickle. Then Katie got on. I caught her eye. I imagined her walking up to Amy and Tara and dismissing them with some cold, witty remark. But it didn't happen. She walked down the aisle, gave me the briefest of sideways glances, and continued on to the backseat.

"Oh, you should leave Hannah alone, Amy," said Tara. "She's so in love with you, she's aching for you."

"Yeah, I know. She's so frigid though, aren't you, Hannah?"

"You know why she's never been with a guy? She doesn't want anyone to find her dick."

"What do you do with it, Han the Man? Do you tuck it into your undies? Oh my God, you can totally see she has a lump there! Look at her thing!"

"I'm going to vomit. That is so disgusting."

"Oh, you know what is disgusting? Jared's haircut! I'm, like, what the fuck happened to your hair?!"

"I know. He said his boss totally made him cut it. So bad…"

And they moved on. For the next ten minutes, they left me alone—until the bus was almost at my stop and I felt something on my back. I ignored it at first. They were clearly trying to get me to turn around. But it kept going. I turned around to see Tara holding a black marker. Amy dissolved into giggles.

"Oh no!" said Tara. "I think you've got ink on your shirt!" The bus pulled into my stop. I stood up and inevitably showed the whole bus the back of my shirt. The shrieks of laughter were utterly predictable, yet still I felt my stomach turn at the sound of it. Her audience was captivated. I put my backpack on in an effort to hide Tara's handiwork, but the damage was well and truly done. It was also posted on Instagram, just in case anyone missed out.

Katie caught up with me after the bus had driven away.

"Hannah, you can't just take that shit."

"What does it say?"

She doesn't answer me.

"Katie?"

"It says 'I have a big dick.'"

I unzipped my backpack and pulled my sweater out. I put it on. I couldn't stand going any farther with those words written on my back.

"You should have slapped her," said Katie.

"You should have slapped her." I was losing it before we even made it home. I wiped and wiped at the tears, but they kept coming.

"What? So it's my fault? Yeah, good one, Hannah."

"They would stop if you told them to!"

"Hannah, Tara is going out with Jared, for fuck's sake. He's my friend. He's Jensen's mate. I don't need this drama. It has nothing to do with me."

"You're supposed to be my sister."

"And so what if I do do something? Then what happens later when I'm not around? What do you think they'll do then?"

"At least they don't pretend they're trying to help me out." I spat the words at her. "I hate you."

Katie rolled her eyes and kept walking. "God, Hannah. Whatever."

———————

I got changed as soon as I was home. I shoved the shirt into a bag and put it in the bottom of the garbage can where Mum wouldn't see it. I did the same with the two other shirts that were ruined in similar ways in the months after that. I told Mum I had lost them, left them behind after swim practice.

FIFTEEN

I AM UP to song 246: "The Lost Art of Keeping a Secret" by a band called Queens of the Stone Age. When I walk around the corner of the agriculture building, Josh is already there. He is down on the grass, next to the porch, crouched beside the paddock fence. A goat has its head through the wire and is eating grass from his hand. He goes to scratch it behind the ear and the goat startles. Josh waits, holding still while the goat watches him, decides he is safe, and reaches forward again to take more grass. Josh looks over his shoulder and sees me. I pull the earphones from my ears.

"I gotta go, Goatee. Or Jane'll get jealous." He stands and vaults up onto the porch, takes a seat on the edge, feet dangling over.

"This is my spot," I say.

"Um, this is out of bounds, Jane. So it's nobody's spot. You can't own it. I'll turn you in. And I think after the whole math prank you pulled, you would be in a lot of trouble." He opens his backpack and pulls out a sausage roll and a carton of chocolate milk.

"Where's your lunch?" he asks me.

I produce a no-name muesli bar.

"Oh, man. That's your lunch? That's all you've got?"

"There was no food left in the house. Again."

"Someone tell World Vision. You could be a sponsor child. Here." He breaks the sausage roll in two and hands me half.

"No, it's OK."

"It is not OK. You need some saturated fats, girl. You'll fade away."

I take the sausage roll from him. We sit there eating our pieces of sausage roll. He is done in two bites.

"How come I get a nickname?" I ask.

"Nickname? What nickname? I have no idea what you're talking about, Jane. Why's it called that anyway? A nickname? Was there some dude called Nicholas and one day someone couldn't be bothered and called him Nick instead? Is human invention fueled by laziness?"

"Couldn't say."

162

"Always ducking around the hard questions, Jane. Very elusive. Drink?" He holds the chocolate milk in my direction.

"No. Thank you."

He shrugs and takes a swig from the carton. "Ahhh, that's more like it. Doesn't your mum make you lunch, Jane? Oh shit. She is around, isn't she? She wasn't in the car accident? Sorry."

"No. She's around. Barely."

"Phew. Man, I get all 'Gah!' when I'm around you." He shakes his hands crazily next to his head. "Scared I'm going to say the wrong thing and traumatize you."

"You won't traumatize me."

"Good. Let's talk about something else. Anything you'd like to discuss?"

"Um. How do you like being at Saint Joseph's? Do…do you feel you are getting a quality education?"

"Ha-ha. Nice reporter voice. Oh man. What is with the teachers here? They're all so concerned. Mr. Black's like, 'How are you settling in, son?'" Josh puts on a fake deep voice, furrowing his eyebrows. "This is right after he gives me a detention. So I'm like, well, it would help if you didn't give me all these detentions. And he gives me extra 'tasks' for industrial arts. I don't even know why. I'll be in class, and he'll hand me a lump of wood and say, 'Go and sand that for me, son.' I mean, is that supposed to be a reward or a punishment? I won't lie, Jane. I find it confusing. And the uniform rules piss me off, I'll be honest. What's with the ties? In summer! Man, it's not a freakin' business college. I'm not here to learn to become a banker."

"What do you want to do? I mean, after Japan."

"You remember that—very observant, Jane." He stretches up, puts his hands behind his head, and leans back against his backpack. "I don't know. I was thinking of design or something. Not graphic design but, like, furniture or something. Like, I'm making this cabinet thing for my industrial arts project. I like furniture."

"It's a reward."

"What?"

"When Mr. Black gives you something extra to do. He's probably noticed you're good at industrial arts."

Josh raises his eyebrows. "You think? I was talking to him about Japanese architecture once—that was cool."

"You're his protégé."

Josh laughs. "But I'm shit at math. He's told me if I want to do design in college, I have to 'buckle down.' But it's just so boring, like who cares about the value of x?"

"I know."

"And what about the textbook questions? If Johnny has to eat eighteen hot dogs, and he's already eaten one-third, how many hot dogs are left? For starters, who the hell is making poor Johnny eat eighteen hot dogs? Secondly, why doesn't Johnny just count them himself? And thirdly, as if that's a problem I'm ever going to have to solve in real life. But I need good grades. So I guess I gotta figure stuff out. Get my shit together. Start giving a crap about Johnny and his hot dogs."

"My dad's an architect."

"Oh yeah? He happy?"

"No. I don't think that's because of his job though."

"Fair enough. I'd like to become an awesome, successful designer mainly so I can stick it to my dad." He laughs. "So I can be all like, 'You said I'd never do anything useful—look at me now!' That makes me really screwed up, doesn't it?"

"I think revenge is a perfectly good motive."

He looks at me and narrows his eyes. "Oh yeah? And who would you like revenge against?"

I don't reply.

He looks at me, waiting. "Hmm, very mysterious, Jane. Let me know if you want me to hurt someone for you. I mean, I can give it a try."

"Your dad wouldn't be happy if you did design in college?"

"My dad is permanently not happy, but yeah. He wants me to be like my brother—wear a suit, make piles of cash, and then spend every Friday getting plastered so I can forget how much I hate my life."

"That's what your brother does?"

"Yeah. And you know, Dad doesn't give a shit about being happy. It's not about that—it's about looking good to everyone else, having an investment property, a nice car, all that crap. Who cares if you want to slit your wrists every waking moment?"

"What about your mum? What does she think?"

"Ah, you see, that's irrelevant because he'll be the one paying for college."

"Oh."

He is quiet for a few minutes. We sit and watch the goats. Eventually, the bell rings for the end of lunch. He turns to me. "Well, it's been swell. Ha. That rhymes. What do you have now?"

"Ah, I have a thing over in D building."

"A thing, huh? Mysterious."

"Yeah."

He laughs. "I'll walk you."

The tourists that bypass our town are usually headed to a village called Leura; it's one of the ones with boutiques and cafés.

It also has a bookstore—the kind I could live in, burrow myself away with Austen and the Brontës. Nestle between Dickens and Hardy. Not a vampire in sight. I was there one Saturday—must have been a month or so before the accident. I remember that because Dad was away at the conference in Switzerland and I felt outnumbered at home without him.

I found a hardcover edition of Hemingway's *The Old Man and the Sea*, printed in 1962—the year my dad was born. It was one of those ones with gilt-edged pages they used to print books on, as if to signal that the words between the covers were important, significant. Useful.

I sat in the corner, between book-lined shelves, and leafed through the book. Whoever had once owned it had treated it as though it were precious. My dad had stacks of books in his study, lots of Hemingway. But I hadn't seen him with a book in his hands for years. His birthday wasn't for another three months, but I bought the book, emptied my bank account. Merilyn, the shop owner, wrapped it in moss-green tissue paper. It's still in that tissue paper, wrapped up and tucked in my bottom drawer.

I left the store and lingered for a moment on the sidewalk, near some tables of the café next door. I was trying to fit the book in my backpack when a waiter came out to take an order from a table. It was Jensen's voice I first recognized. Pathetic really. (Me, that is. Not his voice—it was somewhere between Hugh Jackman and ultimate-fantasy Heathcliff.) The woman at the table said something to him and he laughed, tucked a lock of hair behind his ear. He was wearing black jeans and a black T-shirt, which, can I say, fitted him quite well. Jensen finished taking the order and slipped his notepad into his back pocket before turning toward me to clear a pile of empty plates from another table. I like to think there's a chance I wasn't actually drooling when he saw me.

"Hannah!" That smile again. Warm doesn't quite cover it. "How you doing?"

"Hi. Good."

"What're you up to?"

"Bookstore. I was in the bookstore."

"I love that place. Kind of dangerous working right next to it."

"Ha. Yeah."

"Hey, you want a coffee? I'll make you one. On the house. Sit down."

I sat. He went inside and reemerged a few minutes later with two squat glasses of coffee. The truth is, I had never even drunk coffee before. It was creamy, rich, bitter, and sweet all at once. Jensen sat opposite me. Sighed and rubbed at the back of his neck.

"Started at six this morning. Hectic."

"Ha. Right. I hate that." This coming from someone who had never even had a job at a McDonald's.

"You buy anything?" He nodded toward the bookshop.

"Oh. Um. Yeah." *Use your words, Hannah.* "A Hemingway, old hardback copy. For my dad."

"Lucky him."

"Ha. Yeah."

"Been reading a fair amount of Hemingway in school. We're getting quite acquainted."

Seriously, what guy uses the word *acquainted*? "Yeah, Kate said."

"She mentioned you were into reading. Well, she used the word *obsessed*, if I'm going to be honest."

"Yeah. I guess."

"What you in to?"

"Oh. Me? Austen, the Brontës. If it was written by someone wearing a bonnet, I've probably read it."

He laughed. "What's your fave Austen? I've always been a *Persuasion* man myself."

If Jane Austen herself had come and sat down with us at that point, I'm not sure I would have noticed. What guy reads *Persuasion*?

"How is Kate? I know she's stressing about doing the senior exams this year."

"Senior exams?"

"Yeah." He looked at me, a little crease formed between his eyebrows. "She's doing the exams this year."

It took me a beat too long. I wasn't as good at it as she was.

"Oh, um…"

The frown progressed. I sipped my coffee. I would have changed the topic except anything more than yes or no answers seemed beyond me.

"Hannah?" His mouth curved into an almost grin that didn't match his eyes. "Kate is in her senior year, isn't she?"

"She's a junior. She'll be sixteen next month."

He dropped his gaze to the table. "Well, I bet you think I'm just about the creepiest guy in the universe. Fifteen. In my defense, that's not what she told me."

Fourteen was clearly out of the question in that case.

"No, I don't think…you're creepy."

"Well, I'm starting to… Hey, I've got to get back to it. It's been a pleasure, Hannah. As always."

He stood up, gave a quick smile, and cleared away the glasses.

SIXTEEN

Katie's role models (from pictures stuck on her bulletin board):

* Tavi Gevinson
* Vivienne Westwood
* Kurt Cobain
* Karen O (Yeah Yeah Yeahs)
* Kate Moss
* Alexa Chung
* Our mum (I'm not sure I believe that—she probably added Mum's picture to make herself seem less superficial)

I KNOW SHE's gone, of course. But it's those little reflexes that get me—scanning for her face on the bus after school or expecting the bathroom door to be locked for ages in the mornings while she did her hair and makeup. I can only imagine what it's like for Mum. When she actually cooks dinner, she always makes enough for four. I've seen her standing at the sink after dinner, staring at the remaining portion on the counter, like she wants to cover it in plastic wrap and put it in the fridge for Katie.

Anne asks me to tell her what exactly the Clones used to do to me. I tell her how the graffiti about me being a lesbian went on for months and months, then everyone got bored with that and found new ways to hate me. It was still going on at the start of tenth grade. Once you're targeted like that, it just sticks. I guess every class chooses someone to dump their crap on. They chose me.

The morning that changed everything started out like every other. Katie and I left home to walk to the bus stop at twenty to eight. She was pissed at me because she thought I had told Mum she hadn't eaten any breakfast.

"You're a suck-up." She walked up ahead, yelling at me over her shoulder. "Like it's any of your business anyway."

"Katie, I swear, I didn't say anything."

"Yeah? How did she know I threw it out? She was upstairs. You think she went through the trash?"

"Katie, I didn't say anything."

She stopped walking, turned around. "Listen, you want to screw up your life by being a suck-up? Go for it. Just don't sabotage me while you're at it."

"I didn't. But you should eat breakfast, Katie."

"And what would you know, lard ass? You know, she's going to sit there from now on and watch me eat it. Because of you. Coach says I should slim down. What do you want me to do?"

We both knew that was bullshit. Her expression had changed from one of fury to something else, something softer. Really, I should have guessed what was coming next.

"Look. You have to cover for me with Mum and Dad. I'm not going to school."

"What?"

She dropped her backpack and released her hair from the clip that was holding it up, shook it out over her shoulders. "Jensen's picking me up."

"Now?"

"Yeah. Don't look at me like that, Hannah. He's picking me

up. You're going to write me a fake note next week and say I was at the dentist. Thanks. So I'll see you this afternoon, OK? I'll meet you here at the bus stop. I'll walk home with you."

I stood alone at the bus stop until the bus came up the road. When I got on, there were only a few seats left in the front. I chose one, stowed my backpack on the floor by my feet. The bus doors closed and we lurched onto the road.

The bus drove down the street and rounded a corner. It pulled into another stop. Amy got on, her pixie hair newly bleached, tiny pearl nose stud. It looked like a ripe pimple, not that anyone would ever say that to her. She looked at me and smirked as she walked past, down the aisle. She was followed by Jared, the senior whom Tara and Amy seemed to share between them. He casually stooped down and picked up my backpack as he went by and carried it with him to the back of the bus. "Did you try asking for it back?" my mum would ask later, exasperated. As if Jared had picked it up by mistake. I didn't ask for it back. If you've ever been in a situation like mine, you would know that. I stared straight ahead, the leaden swell of dread growing in my stomach. Maybe they would give my backpack back. Maybe they would just drop it on the ground when they got off the bus, maybe they wouldn't go through my stuff. Maybe if I just concentrated hard enough, I could squeeze my eyes shut and just cease to exist altogether.

There was laughter from the back of the bus. "Awww, gross!" said Jared loudly. I made the mistake of turning around. Jared had opened my bag and was holding up a box of pantie liners. "You got your period, lesbo?" he asked. The whole bus cracked up. Jared put the box back in my bag, zipped it up.

"Don't worry, pig dog. All safe and sound." He gave my backpack a little pat.

When we got to school, everyone filed off the bus. Jared, Tara, Amy, and the little backseat posse were the last to get off. I stood next to the bus, waiting for them; maybe they would just give me my bag back and be done with it. Amy, Tara, and Jared got off. Jared held my backpack high over his head as he went past me. Another bus had pulled in and was spewing out students. The bus stop was crowded and Jared had successfully made sure all eyes were on him. He and Amy started their walk up the sidewalk, toward the gates, ahead of the pack. I could see him, still holding the backpack up, reaching in, grabbing each item one by one, and tossing them on the ground.

I trailed along behind them, picking everything up—science textbook, science notebook, pencil case (contents scattered), school calendar, history textbook, history notebook, wallet, phone (screen shattered), keys, lunch box (contents scattered). There was too much to carry. Things slipped from my arms, falling back to the ground. I didn't cry. Maybe it was like when you go into shock after an accident and can't feel any pain. There was no feeling inside of me.

They didn't leave my backpack, so I had to carry all my stuff to the school office and ask the office ladies if I could have a plastic bag. I told them mine had broken. When I arrived at my locker, there were all the pantie liners, opened, stuck all over the locker door. Aside from the humiliation, I was left with a practical problem. My period was heavy that day. In my mind, I saw a picture of me, blood all over my skirt and my seat. Maybe then they'd all stop the crap about me being a guy.

I peeled all the pads from my locker and put them in the trash.

———————

I was in the hallway—after science, on my way to English— when I passed Charlotte. (I had just finished explaining to my science teacher why I hadn't done my science homework. I didn't tell her my science homework had been spat on and was now on the sidewalk by the bus stop.) I didn't even bother looking at her as we passed, but she grabbed my hand and pressed something into my palm so fast I barely understood what had happened. I turned and saw her walking away through the stream of students without a look back.

I went to my English class and took my seat. When I opened my hand, I saw that she had passed me a tampon.

At lunchtime—in a toilet stall with "Hannah McCann has a dick" written on the walls—I tried to remember the instructions I had once read in a magazine.

"Try to relax; otherwise, it will be more uncomfortable." *Otherwise, it will be more uncomfortable. Otherwise, it will be more uncomfortable. More uncomfortable.*

And the pain was the sharpest thing I had ever felt.

SEVENTEEN

My role models:
* Jane Austen
* Charlotte Brontë
* Emily Brontë
* Miles Franklin
* Virginia Woolf
* Mary Shelley
* Elizabeth Bennet (do fictional people count?)

IF I COULD change one thing, just one, what would I change?

It's the question that keeps me awake at night. I can't even be honest with myself. The answer should be so obvious.

What kind of person does that make me?

Lunch. I am sitting on the porch down at the agriculture plot, same as usual. The air is oven dry. The cicadas are going nuts, and I can't even drown them out with Katie's iPod. Today, I am listening to song number 538, The Cure, "Boys Don't Cry," while I contemplate a particularly unappealing sandwich.

Ten minutes later, I feel the vibration of the porch moving. Josh wanders around the corner, drops his backpack next to mine.

"Afternoon, Jane."

"Hello." I pull an earphone out.

"Jeez, what have you got there?" he asks, eyeing my ham sandwich. "That looks delicious."

The butter has seeped into the bread and dried to a pus-yellow color. I'm pretty sure the ham is almost a week old. Josh pulls a juice box from his backpack, tosses it in my direction. The swirly purple writing declares the juice to be "The Taste of Summer." I thank him, pierce the straw through the hole, and take a sip.

"I already had a sandwich with my mates. You should come sit with us. Not all guys, there's girls too." Josh picks up a pebble, squints, pulls his arm back, and throws it into the paddock. "Hey, haven't seen you at the pool for PE. You been playing hooky?"

"No. I had something else going on."

He frowns.

I hesitate. "I have to…um, I have to go see the school…the school counselor."

"Ohhh, because you're crazy… I'm joking. That's a fair excuse." He picks up another pebble, pitches it toward the paddock. It arcs high into the sky and lands in the grass without a sound. "You ever caught a crayfish?"

"Can't say I have."

"There's a dam down there," he nods toward the gully. "Full of crayfish."

"How do you know?"

"It's common knowledge among truants. Some say the success of the crayfish population is due to the dedicated feeding of the crayfish by the truants."

"OK."

"We should go catch some."

"Truants?"

He laughs. "Crayfish. You can catch them with string."

"And do what with them?"

"Nothing. Just catch 'em."

"The bell's going to ring in five minutes. I've got history."

He makes a face and puts on a ridiculously high voice. "Oh no! I mustn't miss history class. Oh! Oh!"

I throw a twig at him and miss pathetically. He stands up and lifts his bag over his shoulder.

"Well, see ya, Jane. I'm goin' a-crayfish huntin'."

Without even a glance at me, he jumps off the ledge of the porch and begins to stride away, toward the taut wire fence of the paddock. He ducks down, swings his legs through, keeps walking.

"Wait." I stand up. "I'm coming, OK? I'm coming."

"Hurry up then," he yells over his shoulder.

It is cooler down by the trees. And shrill with the sound of cicadas. March flies, their backs gleaming purple, dot the clay banks of the dam. Dragonflies dip at the surface of the flat milky-brown water. It's only when I hear the bell ring that I remember how close we still are to the school.

"You still got that sandwich?" Josh asks, taking a length of string from his pocket.

"Yes."

"Perfect. Can I have it?" He makes a loop in the end of the string, holds his hand out for the sandwich.

"Are you going to catch crayfish with my ham sandwich?"

"We'll see. They might not go for it. Wouldn't be surprised."

I hand it to him; he fiddles with the string and then tosses the bait out into the middle of the pond. He crouches down at the water's edge, the end of the string between his thumb and forefinger. I sit down farther back from the bank. Josh twists the line. He has very long fingers with clean, clipped nails. I can imagine him making things, sanding wood.

"I'm supposed to go up and stay with my dad next school break. He lives in Queensland."

"How long have your parents been divorced?"

"Two years. Dad lives on the Gold Coast with some woman called Sonia. Total bitch. I don't see them much, but last time I went there, I totally pissed Dad off and he told me not to come back."

"He probably doesn't mean it."

"He totally does."

He doesn't say anything for a minute, but his ears turn pink. We sit in silence and watch the water.

"You don't understand," he says eventually. "Sonia is an absolute bitch. Like, literally a total bitch."

"Literally? Your dad's girlfriend is a female dog?"

"Ha. You know what? You're a smart-ass."

"Literally?"

He throws a pebble at me, grins. "Shove it."

A cool breeze winds its way up from the bottom of the gully, blowing stray leaves. They sail down to the ground, speckle the dam.

"My sister's been dead a year next week," I say without really knowing why.

Josh pulls at the line ever so gently. He hooks a stray lock of hair behind his ear. "Must feel weird," he says.

"It does. It feels like a really long and a really short time. I don't know how that works."

"I've never known anyone who died. Even my grandparents are all still hanging in there. Guess I'm lucky."

"Your parents got divorced. That's like somebody dying. I think anyway."

He looks at me. Green eyes. He nods. "You know, you are exactly right. No one ever says that though. They just spin you all this bullshit about how they're actually splitting so you'll be happier."

The string in his hand tugs and goes taut. Slowly Josh stands up. He starts to reel it in, eyes on the water. "Were you hurt, in the accident?"

"Whiplash, a broken ankle. I was in the back."

"Yeah. Right."

He raises his right arm high above his head, gently pulls a slippery blue crayfish away from the water's surface. The crayfish squirms, swinging. Its claws wave around as if it's signaling for help. With a delicate, assured grip, Josh takes it between his thumb and forefinger, holding it just behind the claws. He holds it up in front of his face and grins at it.

"Check out his claws. Man. Could do some damage. Wanna have a cuddle with Hannah, little fella?"

"Don't even think about it."

"Oh, rejected. So harsh. And she doesn't even know you." Josh tosses the crayfish back into the pond. He tears off another bit of sandwich and fastens it to the end of the line.

"You're going to catch another one? So you can just throw it back?"

"What do you want to do? Eat them?"

"Just seems kind of weird, that's all."

"Well, so do you, but you don't hear me going on about it." He flashes me a smile, double-checking I know he's joking. He throws the line into the water and settles back down into position on the bank. We sit there quietly for a few moments, flicking at the flies, watching the pond's surface.

"I knew her, you know. Your sister," Josh says. Somewhere above us, a coachwhip bird calls, its voice a smooth bell note, a drop of cool water.

"How?"

"Oh, you know, parties and that. Would see her around. Everyone thought she was hot, but I guess you know that."

"Hmm."

"She wasn't my type, if it means anything."

"OK."

"I mean, I didn't know her real well. Just knew people who were friends with her. I didn't know she had a sister, that's for sure."

"She kept me pretty separate from the rest of her life."

"You weren't close?"

"No. She was different from me. I don't think she…understood me. She didn't take any crap from anyone. I actually think most people were a little scared of her."

"You used to take a little crap around here, right?"

I nod.

"When I got here, I saw you on your own all the time and I was like, 'Who is that?' and everyone's like, 'Oh, no one hangs out with Hannah.' And I'm like, 'Why the fuck not?'"

"You said that?"

"Ahhh, yeah, I did. Because I don't get it. Katie was a swimmer, wasn't she?"

"Yeah."

"Do you swim?"

"I did. I wasn't as good as her."

"I'm crap in the water."

I laugh.

"Probably drown at the swim meet. I'm serious. Don't get too attached. You a good swimmer?"

"Yeah, I guess. I mean, I used to be."

"You should race. Thorne will make everyone anyway."

"Yeah, no thanks."

"You know, there's this water hole down at the bottom of the gully, really big. We should go there…"

"What, now?"

"Yeah. Go for a swim. Hot enough."

I look back in the direction of the school. "I don't know. I've got English next. I should go…"

"I bet you always do what you're supposed to."

"I'm here, aren't I?"

"Yeah, whatever. I know where I'd rather be."

"I should go."

"Yeah, yeah." He waves at me dismissively.

"See you later." I stand, brush myself off.

As I am walking away, Josh calls after me, "See ya, Jane."

———————

When I got off the bus in the afternoon, Katie was waiting for me. She noticed that I was using a plastic bag instead of my backpack.

"Where's your bag?" she asked.

"They took it."

"What? They took your backpack?"

"No, I'm just carrying my stuff like this for fun."

"Hey, don't get shitty with me about it."

We walked the rest of the way home in silence. I'd hoped to sneak in past Mum without her noticing my lack of a backpack, but it was the first thing she asked me when I walked in the door.

"It broke? I don't understand how it could break so catastrophically that you had to use a plastic bag." She was standing at the juicer making us fresh apple, watermelon, and ginger juice.

"Well, it did."

"Some kids stole it," said Katie.

Mum put down the apple she had poised over the juicer. "Stole it? Who? What happened?" Her tone was more compassionate than I'd expected, and it was enough to make me lose it. I turned away so she wouldn't see my face.

"Hannah? What's going on?"

I went to my room and closed the door. She followed me.

"Can you just leave it? I have homework."

"Hannah, talk to me. What's happening at school?"

"It's nothing."

"It's something. What's going on?"

"Nothing. It was a prank. Some kid took my backpack, that's it."

"Did you ask for it back?"

I didn't answer her. I took my history textbook out of the plastic bag and turned back to my desk.

"Who are you friends with at school?"

"No one."

She laughed. "You must be friends with someone. What about Charlotte? You two have had fights before and worked it out. What's so bad this time?"

"It's complicated."

"Well. Is there another sports team you can join? An activity group at school? Somewhere you can expand your friendship base?"

"I don't play sports. I swim."

"I know you do. I'm just trying to think of some strategies we can use here. If you're in a tricky situation, I'd be looking at changes I could make within myself."

I opened the textbook and uncapped my pen.

"Are you being cyberbullied?" The way she said it made it sound like I was being victimized by a group of robots.

"No."

"Well, you have to help me help you, Hannah. A 'woe is me' attitude isn't going to help. Trust me."

She left the room, closing the door behind her. The tears fell on my page, bleeding the ink from my notes.

Later, when he got home from work, Dad knocked softly on my door. I let him in and he sat on my bed, arms folded.

"Having a bad time at school, Span?"

"I just… I don't fit in anymore."

"It'll pass. I'm not saying it's not bad and I'm not saying that it's easy, but it will pass."

The tears started again.

"Hey, Hannah. Hey, hey." He put his arm around me and I sobbed for what felt like forever. When there was nothing left, he smoothed the hair back from my forehead with his palm. "Can you tell me what's going on?"

I shook my head.

"You being picked on?"

I didn't answer him.

"All right. Well, I'm here when you're ready to talk."

Katie didn't knock, but she did close the door behind her—so I guess that was something. She sat on my bed, picked up my paperback of *Great Expectations*, and opened it.

"'We had looked forward to my one-and-twentieth birthday, with a crowd of speculations and anticipations,'" she read aloud. "Seriously, Hannah. How can you read this stuff? Why doesn't he just say, 'I was excited about turning twenty-one.'"

"He's not excited—he's speculative."

"Speculative."

"Yeah."

She gave a heavy sigh and tossed the book aside. "Was it really awful?"

"Yes."

We sat there with a warm silence around us that I hadn't quite felt with her before. Her gaze didn't go beyond her toes.

"He broke up with me," she said eventually.

"Jensen?"

"Yep. Took me on a picnic and gave me the it's-not-you spiel. Thought he was more imaginative." She picked at a loose thread on my comforter. "Apparently, I'm a really gorgeous girl who he doesn't want to date."

"I'm sorry, Katie."

"Maybe you were right—not quite enough going on up here." She tapped her temple.

"I didn't—"

"Never been dumped before."

"Me neither."

A faint smile. She sniffed, wiped her eyes with the back of her wrist.

"I slept with him, you know. First one. Don't look so surprised. Think I might have been in love with him. What an idiot."

"You're not an idiot, Katie. You're not." I shifted so I was next to her. I put my arm around her shoulders, not sure how she would react. She didn't shake me away.

"So a shit day all around, right?" she said.

"Yeah. A shit day all round."

The next morning, I stood in the doorway, Katie's spare backpack on my back. Katie had already left for the bus stop. I called goodbye to Mum; she was out back on the deck, I think. And I went to step out the door, onto the porch. Twenty to eight, right on time. But I just…couldn't. And it was like the world around me was folding in on itself. And I was folding in on myself. There would be no end to this. No end. And my knees gave way beneath me, and I let myself fold down onto the ground. And if I closed my eyes, curled into a ball, didn't move, didn't speak, I wasn't there at all.

Wasn't there at all.

"Hannah! What's going on? Stand up!"

I wouldn't. I heard her swear under her breath. If Dad had been there, he would have understood what was happening.

But he wasn't. He had already left for work. I didn't open my eyes. Mum physically tried to get me to my feet, but I shook her grip from my arm.

"I'm never going again," I said quietly.

"Don't be silly."

"I'm not going." I got up and went into my bedroom. I closed the door behind me, pushed the desk across it so it wouldn't open. I crawled into bed and listened to her knocking until she gave up.

EIGHTEEN

"Han-nah, Han-nah." Mrs. Van walks across her lawn with her hand on her hip like she's trying to keep it from falling off. "How are you? I haven't seen you for so long. Your mother, she must come out of the house! Oh, Han-nah! Your poor sister, dead and gone."

Mrs. Van is the only person I know who is quite happy to talk about death.

"How is your mother?"

"OK. The same."

"It's not good for her to be inside all day. I tell her to come talk to me, but she won't. I pray for her, Hannah, and for you and your father. Why don't you come inside and I'll make you some nice tea? I make more boterkoek today. For the fair, at the church. Like I have nothing else to do. Do you not see my yard? Do you not see how busy I am?" She shrugs. "But what can I do? Who else will make the boterkoek? No one. At the end, Hannah, we are all on our own."

Yes. According to Mrs. Van, in the end, we will all be on our own, arguing with the lawnmower, making endless cakes, and waiting to die.

Not Katie though.

She takes my elbow and tugs me across the grass. "Come, come."

What am I to do? Left to choose between two lonely women fixated on death. I choose the one with the cake.

———

Mrs. Van's entire house is about the size of our living room. I've been in it before but not for years. She leads me into her sitting room, where there is fluffy brown carpet and two of those big recliner chairs old people seem to adore. She makes me sit down and gets me a cup of tea without asking if I want one. It has about fifteen sugars in it. She puts a slice of cake on the coffee table in front of me and sits down in the other chair. There are photos of smiling people all over her sideboard and walls, some of her grandchildren and lots of black-and-white ones. She points to an old photograph of a tall guy in a uniform. He's totally gorgeous. James Dean gorgeous.

"This is my husband, Joss. He was very handsome. Look how handsome he is."

"He's a hottie, Mrs. Van."

"A hottie." She laughs. "This is good, yes? Yes, he was a hottie, as you say."

"Did he die in the war?"

"The war? No. They try to kill him—he gets shot twice." She holds up two fingers. "But he said to me, 'Hilde, they'll have to do better than that!' No, no. He died fifteen years ago. The cancer. I miss him every day."

She points to a picture of three young girls. "This one is me and these my sisters. This one, Jani, she's still in Holland." She pauses and points to the eldest of the girls. "This, Marieke," she says. She leans forward a little. "You listen to me, Hannah. I know the hurt. And I pray for you every day."

She holds me in her gaze, she doesn't waver. "People say stupid, stupid things when someone you love dies. Rubbish. Nothing gets easier, Hannah. You just go on with life."

She is tiny in her big chair, thin insect limbs. But there is nothing frail about her.

I don't ask her about Marieke. She sips her tea and gazes out at her lawn, probably surveying all the work she still has to do.

"Sometimes it's very hard to go on," she says after a while. "I know this. But we do, don't we?"

I say yes, but I don't know if I really believe it—not every day.

———————

Dinner. Dad cooks steaks on the barbecue. I make a salad. Well, it passes as a salad: a few lettuce leaves, a sliced carrot, and half a grainy tomato from the back of the fridge. (Nanna's due any day now.) Mum doesn't eat anything; she just sits there and looks at the food for fifteen minutes while Dad talks and talks with his mouth full. After a while, he runs out of things to say and we sit in silence. Mum looks up from her plate.

"We should go to the cemetery on the…on Katie's anniversary," she says.

Dad stops chewing.

"The three of us. Yes, that's something we should do." She picks up her fork.

Dad puts his down. "Love, if you want to go, that's fine, that's good. But I…I have a meeting on Thursday."

"You have a meeting on Thursday?"

"Yeah…I've got to meet the Perth manager. It's OK though, love. You go. You and Hannah go."

Mum stares at him, her eyes bright and sharp, drilling. She shakes her head. "I cannot believe you."

"Paula."

"If only we all had a meeting to go to, maybe we could all pretend she's on vacation."

"Paula." Dad's voice is calm, measured. "Paula, not in front of Hannah."

"Not in front of Hannah? Why not? Everything else has happened in front of Hannah!"

I think of Josh's parents. Of his dad on the Gold Coast with a woman called Sonia. I want to get up and leave, but I can't. I am tethered there between them.

"She's got her assessment coming up. They're going to decide whether she remembers what happened or not. So she can tell the court, Andrew—"

"That's enough, Paula."

"Oh, is it? I think so too, Andrew. I think we've all had enough. But we don't have a choice, do we?"

My dad closes his eyes, takes a deep breath. He crosses his long arms, the arms that he used to wrap around my mother. Folds them across his chest.

"Well, some of us don't anyway," she says.

NINETEEN

JOSH SETS A cold bottle of juice down next to me.

"How much was it?" I ask.

"It's all good. I gotta deal going with the cafeteria lady." He winks at me.

"I really do not want to know."

"Just happy to reap the benefits, are you? Typical." Josh sips his Coke. His shirt is crumpled and untucked, as usual. Tie nowhere to be seen. He unzips his backpack and pulls out a book. *The Hunger Games.*

"You like books? Read this? It's good. No pictures of Jennifer Lawrence though. Which is a shame. I finished it in, like, a week. What? You look shocked. I can read, you know. Just don't tell Black. You'll ruin my reputation."

"You like him, don't you?"

"Black?"

"Yeah. I think you're quite fond of him."

"'Fond'? What the hell? You are Jane Eyre."

"I'm just saying, I think you…respect him more than you let on."

"Yeah, well. At least he gives a shit if I don't do my home-work." He looks away, takes another swig of Coke. "You know, there's a whole other world beyond this porch. There's like space and trees and other places to sit and even other people—crazy, I know. Some of them are actually friendly. Ever think of venturing out?"

"No."

"You afraid of them, Janie?"

"No. I'm really not. I just… I like it here."

"Don't want anyone's pity?"

"Exactly."

"Yeah, well. You don't have mine. Except when it comes to your sandwich-making skills." He takes a piece of paper from his pocket and unfolds it. The crossword. "With the unstable lawyers? Six letters. Third letter *f*."

"Um…infirm."

"Well, that's just ridiculous. How do you do that?"

"Not sure… Was it better after your dad left? I mean, was it a relief that the tension was gone or something?"

"No, it wasn't a relief. That's what they want you to think though. As if two Christmases is compensation for a fucking family." He pauses, flicks the pen between his fingers. "My mum goes on dates now. She's decided she's ready to 'get back into life.' As if going out for Chinese with some pathetic, balding creep is getting into life. Do you know how weird that is?" He laughs, but it clearly isn't funny. "I have to meet these guys who come to my house to pick up my mum. 'Hello there, young man. My name's John. I'm a prick. Why else would I be single?' You know what she said to me? She told me that she's still a woman with needs. Those are words you don't want to hear coming from your mum's mouth." He sighs. "So, short answer, no, it's not better."

"I think my mum would be too depressed to go on dates. And Dad's pretty much a cripple now…"

"So he'd need to go out with someone who could, like, carry him? That's awkward on a first date."

"Yeah. True."

"I don't get it, Jane."

"Don't get what?"

"I don't understand why you used to get teased. You seem all right to me."

"No one else thinks that. I'm too serious. I take things too seriously, and I've got a stick up my butt."

He cracks up. "Sorry, I don't mean to make fun of your problems." He bites his lip, watches me. "You're serious, sure. But that's a good thing. You take people seriously, Hannah. You listen." He pushes his hands through his hair and leans back against the wall. "Do you know how rare that is? Most people just wait till the other person finishes so they can talk about themselves again. It pisses me off. They don't listen. But you…" He looks away. "You act like the way I feel is important. You make me feel valid."

"OK. Thank you."

"You're welcome." He clears his throat and takes a pen from his pocket. "Moving on to: Henry. Four letters."

"Ford."

"You see, this is why I hang out with you, Jane."

———

Anne hands me a mug of jasmine tea.

"I'd give you something stronger, but I'd lose my job," she says. She sits opposite me and picks up her notepad. "Remember what I said: no talk about the weather, although it is appallingly hot."

"Yeah, it is."

"I heard a rumor—and this is crazy—that you might have a friend here. An actual friend. That true or am I being gullible and optimistic?"

204

"It might be true. I guess."

"A male friend."

"He's not my boyfriend."

"Do you want him to be?"

Katie chips in, *Don't ask Hannah about guys—she'll freak out.*

"Um, I don't really see why I have to talk about that."

She smiles. "Wait. Have I found something you're even less eager to talk about than the car accident? Is that possible?"

"Maybe."

"Great, well, let's talk about the car accident, since you're so eager. There's going to be a hearing soon. Yes?"

"Yes."

"And as a witness, the police want to question you at the trial."

"Yes."

"Under oath. But you need a psych assessment first."

"Yes."

"You haven't given them any information."

I look at her and she does the same old thing and looks right back at me, unflinching. "I don't remember."

"Sometimes, when faced with really traumatic stuff, our minds sort of shut down to protect themselves. You've heard that before?"

"Yes."

"I think maybe that's what's happening to you."

"I hit my head."

Anne shrugs. "Sure. But with most concussions, when the person hasn't been knocked unconscious, the missing pieces fall back into place after a while. That hasn't happened for you, has it?"

I don't answer her.

"You know, when you're ready, you might start to remember things, Hannah. I want you to be prepared for that."

How do you get ready for that?

"Hey, Jane."

The last bell of the day has rung, and students spill out of classrooms and head toward the buses. A mass exodus. Josh stands in front of me, blocking the flow of people and forcing everyone to go around us.

"How are you?" he asks.

"Um, good. But I need to get the bus."

"No, see, you should come to the skate park. There's a bunch of us going. Take a load off, see me attempt a kickflip three-sixty—it'll change your life."

"Change my life?"

"Yeah, the sheer beauty of it will change your perceptions of the world, Jane. You will never see a skateboarder more average than myself."

"I'm supposed to come and watch you skate?"

"Yeah. Bring me snacks and stuff."

"How liberating."

"Very. There'll be other girls there. You can talk about how cute I am. Seriously, come hang out. Talk to some other humans. You might like it. I know you've got your whole solitary-confinement thing going on, but you might actually not have a horrible time."

Soon, my bus will arrive and open its doors, ready to take me off into another afternoon of predictability. Safe predictability.

"Janie, come on. Offer is closing."

"OK."

"OK?"

"But I'm not bringing you drinks."

"We'll see. To the parking lot, Jane. Sammy awaits."

"Sammy?"

"Sam Wilks. You know him? No, you don't know him. He's a senior. Lives next door to me. Has a ride, which means I have a ride, which means you have a ride. One of the many benefits of being mates with me, 'cause you seem to need reminding. You're getting that drill sergeant look in your eyes. It's not a stolen car, Jane. We're not joy riding. It's Sammy's mum's station wagon. A Volvo for frig's sake. C'mon, move those feet, sister."

When we get to the parking lot, I see that Sam Wilks is leaning on the driver's door of what is indeed a Volvo station wagon. His school uniform is even less…uniform than Josh's. He has a shaved head and about six holes in each ear, which he is methodically filling with earrings dug out from his shirt pocket.

"Little tardy there, Joshy," he says. "Gotta get going. Workin' tonight." He looks up, squints a little in my direction. "Hannah, yeah? I'm Sam. Get in. And you"—he points at Josh—"no eating in the car. You get crumbs on the seats and my mum will kill me. I don't need that crap, man."

Josh gives him a salute.

"And you guys are gonna have to squish up in the back, OK? Got Mark and Ollie comin' too. If they friggin' hurry up."

Mark and Ollie do turn up right as Sam is starting the car. They are ex–Reacher Street, like Josh. One of them (I don't know which) is drinking a cup of iced coffee, which Sam makes him finish before getting in the car. Perhaps sensing my reluctance to be squished between two guys, Josh offers to take the middle seat. I slide in next to him and our shoulders touch. When we leave the parking lot, Sam drives at a pace that would put most grandmas to shame.

I send Mum a text: Be home later, going to skate park. If she bothers to read it, she will probably think it's Katie's ghost texting her.

It's probably not much of a surprise to hear that I haven't spent a whole lot of time hanging around the skate park (or loitering, as the case may be). I discovered after exiting Sam's car that it is not the debauched drug den the local paper predicted it would be when it opened. On this particular afternoon though, it does seem to be a popular hangout for teenagers whose fake IDs were used at the bowling alley long ago. Josh seems to know most of them. He must notice my face when I spot a group featuring a few Clones because he says in my ear, "Don't worry, Jane. Those punks give you any grief and I'll give 'em a kickflip to the head. Just give me time to practice first."

There're two ex–Reacher Street girls who came to Saint Joseph's at the same time as Josh. They sit on the concrete in the shade and give Josh a wave. He goes over to them and I follow, trying not to feel like the lost puppy that used to follow Charlotte around.

"Ladies," he says by way of a greeting. Maddie, whom I recognize from my English class, rolls her eyes in a way that is more friendly than anything else.

"Afternoon, Joshua."

Maddie has wild, curly hair like Katie's was, and I notice her blue school skirt has been hemmed with bright-red thread.

"You bring food?" the other asks. She's Asian and very beautiful, straight black hair to her waist.

"Yes, Lola. You're lucky I haven't eaten it. You know what Sammy's like with his car."

"Oh, she knows," says Maddie.

Lola gives her a death look. "One more word, Maddie, and I will hurt you."

Maddie holds up her palms in surrender.

Lola looks at me and smiles. "Hannah, right? I'm Lola. Way to go with the introductions, Josh."

He's not listening—too busy watching Sam attempt a jump that looks like it could end in death.

"Hi."

"Hi. Sit." They both slide over to make room in the shade.

"So Josh has dragged you along to watch," Maddie says.

"Something like that."

"Always desperate for an audience."

"Poor guy," says Lola.

Josh turns. "At least wait till I'm out of earshot."

I sit next to Maddie and Lola, and neither seems to mind that I am mostly silent. Josh, as it turns out, is more gifted with a skateboard than I'd expected, and while he's skating, Maddie raids his backpack and finds a bag of corn chips.

"So what's the deal with you and Josh?" she asks, offering me a chip.

"Like it's your business!" says Lola. She turns to me. "Maddie and Josh were, like, married for two years. Now she acts like she's his mother."

"I do not! I'm just asking."

"We're not together or anything," I say carefully.

Maddie smiles and shakes her head, her hand on my shoulder. "Lola's talking about ages ago. There's no problem. I'm just curious."

"Like I said," says Lola, "she thinks she's his mother."

"Would you shut up? I'm trying to have a civilized conversation here."

"You're interrogating the poor girl. Ignore her, Hannah."

"Should we talk about Sam Wilks then, Lola?"

"Arghhh, shut up!"

"Look, Hannah, I'm not interrogating you. It's just, I've known Josh a long time. Promise me you won't break his heart?"

I can't imagine having the capability of breaking anyone's heart.

"Oh God, you look scared. I'm not saying anything! Relax!"

"I told you not to threaten her," says Lola.

"I'm not! I didn't!"

"It's OK," I say. "I understand. There's really nothing going on, he's just... We're friends."

"I know. Sorry."

"Like I said, you think you're his mum," says Lola, offering me a Whopper, which is also from Josh's backpack.

"Do not."

"Do too. You need therapy."

"Most people need therapy," I say, and this seems to go over pretty well.

———

Sam Wilks pulls the station wagon up in front of my house. I get out and Josh follows me. He hands me my backpack, walks around, and leans on the back of the car, maybe in an attempt to get out of earshot. He folds his arms and looks at me, right at me.

"I like you, Hannah."

His eyes really are very green.

"I know you think you're the most screwed-up person in the world—maybe you are—but I want you to know that I like you and that everyone is screwed up to some degree. I'm not going anywhere, OK? I don't expect anything from you. I just want you to know that."

"OK." My voice is barely a whisper. "I'll see you later, OK?"

"OK." He grins. "You've gotta stop being such a flirt. It's killing me."

———

Mum comes out of her bedroom as I step through the front

door. I wonder if maybe she is going to ask who my friends are, who gave me a lift home. She doesn't.

Later, I am in my room when the doorbell rings. I go out to answer it, but my mother is already there. Mrs. Van stands on our doorstep. I watch from behind my mother. She doesn't know I am there.

"We don't need more cake, Mrs. Van," she says.

"I am not bringing you cake. Here." She leans down and picks something up. A plant in a plastic pot. "It is an orchid."

My mother doesn't say anything.

"Take it. Plant it. It will be good for you. It will be purple when it flowers. Katie told me she liked my orchids."

That would have been a Christmas-cash ploy. "Take it."

My mother rubs her forehead and sighs.

"Why don't you want it? Tell me."

"You're always bringing me things. I don't need things."

"You need this plant. You need to plant it."

"What? Am I supposed to remember her with a plant? Is that the idea? I'm supposed to be content with the fact that I have lost my daughter now that I have this stupid plant? Why do you think something like this is a substitute for my daughter?"

"You didn't lose her," Mrs. Van says. "It isn't your fault. Do you think I am an idiot? This plant is not supposed to be a substitute. No! You plant it outside, in your garden—"

"It's Andrew's garden."

"You plant it in your garden. You go outside every day into the sunshine, and you water it, you pull out the weeds. If you can't do anything else, this is OK. All you do every day is water your plant. If you can do that for two weeks, I will bring you another. Take it, go on."

"I don't think I want it."

Mrs. Van sets the pot down on the doorstep. "You should talk to me."

"What?"

"You must talk to somebody. I am right here."

"Go away."

"I did not hear you."

"*Go away!*"

"Aha! That is it. You want to shout and yell? You shout and yell at me. I am a tough old woman, I can take it. You can't keep it all inside here." She points to her chest. "It will dry you up and you will be no use to anybody."

Mum says nothing.

Mrs. Van stares up at her, squinting through her glasses. She picks up the plant and hands it to my mother. "Water it. It will flower next winter."

It takes me a moment to realize Mum is crying.

TWENTY

DVDs on Katie's bookshelf:
- Breaking Bad box set
- Six Feet Under box set
- Friends box set
- Breakfast at Tiffany's
- Rear Window
- Carrie (original version)
- Pulp Fiction
- Project Runway (seasons three to five)
- The September Issue
- Trainspotting
- Psycho (original version)

* The Birds
* Sex in the City box set

WEDNESDAY. THERE IS heat in the day before there're even shadows on the ground. A creamy brown clog of smoke haze hangs in the air. My bus pulls into the bus area and most people are silent, feet heavy, knowing the revolting day that's in store: airless classrooms, useless ceiling fans, morning assembly in a sun that could ignite us.

I have been awake most of the night. Not for the usual reasons. And there is a twist in my stomach that's different than all the other ones that have been there before. I realize I might actually be looking forward to the day.

I leave the bus, begin the walk up the hill to the quadrangle. Other students straggle up the sidewalk. A small cluster sits by a clump of grevilleas. They are in my grade. Some of them were at the skate park yesterday, Josh's friends or the people he's friends with when he's not doing the crossword at the agriculture plot. Maddie and Lola are there. So are Charlotte and Tara.

"Hey, Hannah!" one of the guys calls out.

I turn.

"It's Hannah, right?" He has short dreadlocks, fierce eyes.

"Yeah."

"What you up to with our Joshy, huh?"

Charlotte nudges him, shakes her head. He shrugs her away.

"He sez you guys are getting to know each other pretty well."

I swallow. There is breath—there is breath somewhere inside me, but I can't get at it.

"Sez you're a very talented young lady."

"Nick, shut up," Maddie says.

The boy laughs. "I'm just trying to make friends!"

"You're a dick."

"Yeah, but what a dick."

I am walking. I am walking away, but it feels as though I'm not moving at all. There are footsteps behind me, someone touches my shoulder. It's Maddie.

"Are you OK? Ignore Nick. He's an asshole. You OK?"

I nod. I don't know what to do with this. I do not know what to do with it.

———

Josh follows me out of roll call. "Fishing trip today, Jane Eyre? I'm thinking third period, math."

"Can't." I walk faster.

"Why?"

"I just can't."

"Janie—"

I stop. "Leave me alone."

People hear, they pause, look, then keep walking.

"What?" The confusion in his eyes almost makes me change my mind.

"Just leave me alone."

"Jane, what's up? Is this about yesterday? Um, can I say I was drunk and to forget what I said? Will that help?"

"My name is Hannah. But you know that, don't you? Told your friends. Told them all kinds of stuff. What else are you going to say about me?"

He grabs my hand. I try to pull away, but he pulls back, steers me into an empty classroom.

"Let go of me!"

"Hannah, what the fuck?"

"What else are you going to say about me, Josh?"

"I don't know what you're talking about."

"Leave me alone."

He keeps hold of my hand. Frowns at me.

I pull away, leaving him there.

———————

At the end of second period, I leave English class and begin the walk across the yard toward the agriculture plot. After what happened this morning, I can't shake my craving for solitude. As I am walking, I notice that the yard seems almost entirely empty of students. There is noise though, like a crowd watching a sporting event. It comes from the direction of the cafeteria. As I near it, I see the backs of students as they scuffle and strain to get a closer look.

It's obviously been going on for a while because both their school uniforms are torn and smudged with dirt. Josh has Nick, the dreadlocks guy, by the collar. He rams him against a concrete pillar. Nick takes a swing, connects with Josh's chin. Josh staggers back a step, barely losing a second before returning a punch, which sends Nick to the ground. Josh is on him then, holding him by the collar, shouting. Which is when three male teachers, one of them Mr. Black, finally arrive, whistles shrieking. It takes two of them to pull Josh away—there is blood streaming from his left eyebrow. Another teacher pulls Nick to his feet, and as soon as he's upright, Josh tries to take another lunge at him. There's more shouting, this time from the teachers, and it's as they're hauling Josh and Nick away that Josh's eyes meet mine. He holds my gaze.

I don't see him for the rest of the day.

———————

On Thursday morning Mr. Black pulls me aside on my way into homeroom. He tells me Josh has been suspended for two days. He asks me what I saw and I tell him.

"So you don't have any idea who instigated the fight?" he asks. "Who punched who first?"

"No," I answer. "I wasn't there when it started."

"Your name was mentioned apparently."

"I don't know anything about it."

He looks at me skeptically. "All right. Go to your seat."

Mum knocked on my door. "Hannah? Darling, can you open up?"

If I pulled my knees up to my chin, wrapped my arms around my legs, and closed my eyes, it was like I wasn't there at all. The very act of opening my eyes only anchored me in reality, and I didn't want to be in my reality anymore. I was done.

I could hear Mum on the phone with Mr. Black. She didn't talk to him so much as shout. She demanded to know what the school was doing about the bullying. She demanded suspensions, expulsions, criminal charges, public flogging—you name it. Then she phoned my dad and then Nanna. From the sound of things, Nanna's solution was that I drop out of school and get a floristry apprenticeship.

I don't remember the rest of the day very well. At some point, I moved to the window and lay there looking up at the sky. I didn't do anything else. I wasn't sure I could, and I didn't have the energy to try. In the evening, after he got home, Dad knocked softly on my door. I heard Mum follow him down the hallway. "Just let me talk to her," he said. I listened to him knock, but I didn't move. Eventually, he spoke. "Spannie, I'm just going to sit on the floor here, on the other side of the door, so I'm here when you need me."

I don't know how long I waited before I got up and pulled the desk away from the door. He came into my room and sat beside me on the bed.

"You've got to let us help you, honey."

"Anything you do will make it worse."

"Make what worse? Talk to me, Span."

But I couldn't.

On Friday, I round the corner of the agriculture building and Josh is on the porch, ripped shorts and a tank top, no shoes. He lies on his back, hands behind his head, eyes closed. I find myself noticing his bronzed upper arms. He has useful-looking shoulders. Josh opens one eye. Closes it again.

"Nick Pergis is a tool, Hannah. How come everyone else knows not to trust a fucking thing that comes out of his mouth but not you?"

I sit on the edge of the porch, dangle my legs over. "You didn't have to punch him."

"You don't get to tell me what I should and shouldn't do."

"Sorry."

He sits up, eyes burning into me. "Do you really think I would say something like that about you? Do you, Hannah?"

"Josh. I'm sorry. He caught me off guard. I'm not…"

"Not what?"

"Not good at trusting people."

"You don't say."

"You don't understand," I whisper.

He watches me.

"You don't know what it was like before…before my sister died. The stuff they used to do."

"I'm not them."

"I know."

I wonder if he will get up and walk away, but he doesn't.

"Are you in trouble?" I ask after a few moments.

"They gave me two days' suspension. First warning for fighting. Two counts and you're out. Seems a little harsh to me—most people want to punch Nick in the head at one time or another."

He looks away. He has an expression I haven't seen on him before. Hurt.

"I'm sorry, Josh."

He turns his face to me. Examines mine, unsmiling.

I can feel myself blushing.

"Yeah, well. You're lucky I'm an awesome guy. Very forgiving." An almost smile.

"Thought you were a peaceful kind of a guy."

"Ha. Almost got expelled from my last school for fighting. Thought I was over it though. Obviously not. Don't really see what the big deal is—if you're both up for it, I mean."

"What did your mum say?"

"Said she's going to send me to my dad's. Standard response from split parents. What do the ones who are still married threaten you with? Boarding school?"

"I haven't been caught fighting. Couldn't really say."

"Saw a movie about a boarding school once, girls' one. They seemed to have a pretty good time. Interesting dress code."

"Oh, shut up."

"By the way, you know you're skipping class right now? Bell rang a long time ago."

"Did it?"

"Yeah. But you're here now, so…" He shrugs. "Since you're already on the slippery slide to doom, might as well make the most of it. I'm going for a swim. Coming?"

"I don't know."

"Come on, Jane. It's freakin' boiling. Can you imagine Rourke in this weather? She'll be a madwoman. She's probably brought a weapon to class."

"I'm not on suspension though."

"You will be soon if you keep hanging around with me."

"I'll come, but I'm not swimming."

"We'll see, Jane Eyre."

"Why do you call me that?"

"Can't remember your real name. Helen? Heather? Hayley?"

"Oh, shut up."

The bush hums as we wind down the side of the gully. There must have been a fire here not long ago—tree trunks are scorched charcoal, their regrowth a shock of acid green. The new leaves start at the base of the trunk and feather out, all the way up the branches, making the trees look like giant, tentacled creatures rising up from the earth.

"How much farther?" I ask.

Josh is ahead of me, picking his way through the rocks. "A ways. Down at the bottom. Listen."

I strain my ears to sift through the hiss of the cicadas. I can just make out the rushing of water. Using the rocks like the steps of an amphitheater, we make our way deeper into the gully. The opposite side looms taller and taller as we go down, and I have the feeling of being folded into the spine of a great, lush book. The rush of water intensifies, and soon, I can feel the dampness on my skin and see a sandy bank through the trees. A wide flow of dark sparkling water gushes around hunks of rock.

Josh heads downstream, along a narrow goat track by the water. I follow. Soft grass overhangs, stroking the running water. Beneath the surface, the smooth, flat stones are silver and copper. We step over a boulder, and then I can see where the stream leads to a big shimmering body of water, four times the size of a backyard pool.

"Told you it was worth it." Josh pulls his tank top over his head. I can feel myself blushing again. It's fair to say he looks like he gets a good deal of exercise. He starts to climb a track that leads back into the bushes.

"Where are you going?"

"Up there." He points to a rocky ledge at the top of a cliff face. The drop into the water is about ten yards.

"No way," I say.

"Yeah. You have to try it."

"I'll pass."

Josh shrugs, follows the well-worn path, hoists himself up

one rock face, then another. I hesitate and then start to follow. He glances over his shoulder, gives me a grin.

"This doesn't mean I'm jumping," I say.

"Yeah, yeah."

We get to the top. It is a huge slab of rock, like a balcony overlooking the water. Josh doesn't even walk to the edge and peer over; instead, he runs, taking three quick strides, and launches himself into the air. He lets out a whoop as he drops from sight. Then there is the smack of his body hitting the water below. I walk gingerly to the edge and peer over. The water's surface is unsettled, but I can't see Josh.

"Josh?"

A hot rush comes up the back of my neck. I wait. "Josh?"

Nothing. Not even bubbles. I scream his name. I kick off my shoes. There is no time for the tie. No time even for a deep breath. I leap from the edge of the rock. There is air rushing past my face and the water coming toward me and then it is in my ears and eyes—nothing but green. The cold prickles my scalp. I lunge in the direction I hope is up, lungs aching from the shock of the drop and the cold and not enough air. I break through the surface, gasping, look left and right and behind. Nothing but rippling water and still, silent bush. I dive back under, but I can't see anything, not even knowing which direction to look. I come back up to the surface.

"Josh?"

And then there is laughter. Josh steps out from behind a boulder on the bank.

"Whoa, I didn't expect you to jump in! I'm touched. No, really." He laughs so hard, he doubles over, hands on his knees.

My breath catches. I turn and swim to a rock, realize I still have my socks on.

"Oh, come on. That was hilarious."

"You shouldn't have done that."

I hoist myself out of the water, the rock's surface grazing my palms. Without looking back, I head in the direction of the track, back up the gully. There is a pulling and churning in my guts. My lungs feel like someone is squeezing them.

"Hannah?! Come on, Han. I'm sorry. Hannah! Come back."

I pick up my backpack, keep walking.

Josh runs up from behind me and ducks in front. "Come on, Han." He laughs.

I turn my head away, but he sees my face.

His smile vanishes. "Oh shit. Hannah, I'm sorry, I didn't… Oh shit, I'm sorry."

"You shouldn't have done that." Water drips from my hair. A hot, sour gush of sickness comes up from my stomach. I turn away and vomit into the sand.

"Are you OK? Shit. Are you all right?"

Embarrassed and furious, I wipe my hand across my mouth. A deep breath pushes into my chest.

"Han. I'm sorry. I was just kidding around. I didn't expect... Are you OK? I'm sorry."

I keep my hand clamped over my mouth and try to breathe deeply through my nose. I let my knees fold beneath me.

Josh grabs my elbows. "Hey, hey." He steadies me, eases me to the ground.

I sit in the sand and put my face in my hands.

He crouches down next to me and puts an arm around my shoulders, hugs me toward him. "It's OK," he whispers. "I'm OK."

I put my head on his chest and let him hold me. We sit there on the ground until I stop shaking.

———

When I get home from school, my mother is sitting in the living room. The television isn't on. The radio isn't on. She isn't reading a book or even looking out the window. She is looking at nothing and I step through the door and she turns her eyes to me.

"Hi," I venture. She says nothing. I walk past her into the kitchen. She follows me.

"The school called," she says.

228

I open the fridge. The glass shelves gleam with Spray 'n' Wipe. Nanna must have been around.

"It was your counselor actually."

I stop. "Why?"

"She said you didn't make it to your appointment today—you didn't go to class either. Is that right?"

"I guess."

"Where were you?"

I turn away and head down the hall.

She follows. "Where were you, Hannah? Is your hair wet?"

I turn and face her. "Are you and Dad getting divorced?"

"What? Hannah, we're not talking about that. I'm asking you why you missed school today. You're not in trouble. I just want to know why."

"Why do you care?"

"I beg your pardon, young lady."

"You don't care about anything. Why do you suddenly care about school? You wouldn't notice if I dropped out. How would you even know? You're always in bed." It is the most I have said to her for nearly a year.

"Hannah!"

"Are you and Dad getting divorced?"

"Come and sit down," she says, pointing toward the living room.

229

"No."

"Why do you think we're getting divorced?"

"Because you hate Dad."

"I don't hate anyone."

"Yes, you do. You hate Dad because of the accident. You think he killed Katie."

"Hannah, honestly, I don't know what to think."

"You think it was all his fault. It wasn't. You weren't there."

"Why don't you tell me then? Tell me what happened."

"*I don't remember!* But I know it wasn't his fault!"

She doesn't say anything.

"You don't care about anything else! It's all about you and how sad you are. I was there. I'm the one who watched her die."

I think she might cry at that. But she doesn't. "You said you don't remember anything. If you remember, you have to tell the police."

"Fuck you."

I push past her and go into my bedroom. I slam the door and slide down to the floor, close my eyes. I shake my head, but I can't get it out—I can see it. I can see it behind my eyes, the picture that forms in the black of my memory. I see the intersection. I hear the sound. Katie's eyes look into mine, utterly terrified.

I can't be near her, can't be in the house. I open the window and push out the screen. I climb out into our front yard. The heat outside welcomes me, envelops me. Mrs. Van is in her yard. She sees me and calls out. I ignore her and keep walking. I walk down the road, on the edge, where the asphalt breaks into ochre pebbles and dust. Somewhere in the distance, a fire truck wails. I climb the hill and turn onto Blue Gum Crescent, lined with brick houses, steel fences. There is the splash and squeal of kids in a backyard swimming pool. I head down Blue Gum, turn onto the highway, and follow the sidewalk. I walk and walk until I get to Johnson Street. It takes forever. My shirt is clinging to my back; sweat trickles from my temples. The cars sweep down the slope of the hill, tinted windows up, passengers freshly chilled with air-conditioning. I walk to the edge of the road. There is a speed limit sign there that says fifty. Taped to the traffic light pole is another bunch of tiger lilies, the cellophane that wraps them quivers and flutters with every passing car. I stand there with my toes on the lip of the curb and feel the push of air from the traffic, like it could pick me up. A car blasts its horn in warning. Another. Another. I watch as a semitrailer approaches the intersection two hundred yards farther up the hill. It thunders, hurtles toward me. The horn bellows. I can see the blue sky reflected in its windshield, the sunlight flare on the chrome grill. The wind takes my hair and whips my cheeks. I step from the curb, back onto the grass of the embankment.

TWENTY-ONE

THERE IS A cuckoo clock on the wall, a tiny wooden house with flowers carved into its eaves and a front door painted china blue.

"From Holland," Mrs. Van says as she places a glass of water in front of me. "My sister, Jani, send it for my birthday, many years ago. Too many!"

She nestles into her chair opposite me. I tell her it looks comfortable, more for something to say rather than because it does.

"It is a ridiculous chair. My son buys it for me, tells me it will lift me up to my feet, save my back. See this lever here? I tell you, I pull it and I go shooting through the window. Ridiculous chair."

I laugh and she frowns at me.

"You think it is funny to catapult an old woman out the window. Young people all the same. My sister, Marieke, she was always making trouble for the old people. She would ring their doorbells and then run away or meow like a cat in their window. She was fearless." Mrs. Van shrugs. "Or stupid, either way."

She sips her tea and gazes at the clock. "Marieke, she has been gone seventy-four years. She would be an old woman now herself." Mrs. Van laughs softly. "I cannot imagine that."

"Did she die in the war?"

"Yes. She used to lead the youth group at the church. The Germans occupied Holland. But they had left our village alone mostly. This one day, there were rumors, you know, of the Germans nearby. The Dutch police and authorities, you understand, they did whatever the Nazis wanted. They had surrendered to them." She closes her eyes and shakes her head. "Nobody knew what was going to happen—everyone was scared. It was the day of the youth group meeting and I said to her, 'Marieke, you cannot go. It is not safe'—the Germans, you see, did not like people meeting in groups, no matter if they were just teenagers. They would arrest people for talking too long on the street. But she was so stubborn. Defiant. She would have wanted to meet, especially to spite the Germans. Silly, silly girl. So she went. And an hour later, my neighbor comes to the door and tells me the Germans are on the way into our village. So I run—I run down the hill, across the bridge to the church." She shrugs. "But I am too late. People there, they tell me the Nazis have arrested all the teenagers for conspiring. Except Marieke. And I say, 'Where is my sister?' and they tell me she tried to stop the Germans. I go into the church hall and I find her in the doorway. She tried to block them. To stop them taking the others…" Mrs. Van pauses. "She must have thought they wouldn't shoot a girl. She was wrong."

There is nothing to say. I hold the glass in my hand and let the water warm.

"People, they say to me, 'How can you believe in a God who would let this happen?' But, Hannah, this is why I believe in God. Because, otherwise, what is there? Only death and pain. And it is meaningless. I cannot accept this. I cannot accept that my sister is no different to a bug squashed under a shoe. There will be justice. But it will not be on this earth. I was very, very angry for a long time, Hannah. Even after we had settled here and I had my own family. But the anger—it would have killed me too if I had not learned…if I had not learned to live despite what happened to my sister."

I swallow and look at the glass in my hands.

"You need your mother."

"It's not her fault," I whisper.

The night after I refused to go to school, I lay in bed listening to my parents talking.

"I can't help her if she won't talk to me," Mum said.

"Obviously it's not easy for her to talk about."

"I get that. I'm not stupid, Andrew."

"I'm not saying you are. I'm just saying we have to be gentle with her. She's just that kind of kid."

"I know my daughter."

"Hey, why are you getting defensive?"

"I'm just worried about her. This isn't a solution to what-ever's going on. Not talking about it and barricading herself in her room isn't a solution."

"She's being bullied."

"Who would bully her? Why?"

"I don't know, but I'm certain that's what's going on."

"She can't stay home tomorrow. The longer she stays home, the harder it'll get. I'll call her homeroom teacher again tomorrow."

When I woke up in the morning, my mother had taken my uniform from my closet and laid it on the end of my bed: short-sleeved shirt, plaid skirt, bottle-green socks.

"Come on, Hannah," she said. "You can do this."

She had turned on my light, opened the curtains so sunshine flooded into my bedroom. I burrowed farther down under the covers. She peeled them back.

"I'm going to call the school and have a talk with Mr. Black. But you need to get up. Come on, I'll get your breakfast."

She left the room, and I pulled the covers back up over my head, curled into a ball. Five minutes later, she returned. "Hannah! Come on, sweetheart. You're going to miss the bus. Honey, you can't stay home. Whatever it is, hiding in bed isn't going to help. Come on."

"Hannah!" Katie yelled from the hall. "We're late. Hurry the puck up."

My mother sighed. "Yes, thank you, Katherine." She sat on the edge of the bed. "We're going to figure this out, OK?" She patted my leg. "You can do this. You're not alone. Whatever it is, we'll fix it. But you have to get back on the horse."

I lay there, tears running down my nose. I wanted to get on the horse and gallop away. I didn't move. I thought she would give up, but she didn't. She stayed there, sitting at my feet on the bed.

"Hannah, I know this is hard. I do," she said. She didn't know. She had no idea.

Dad looked in the doorway. "Paula, I'll take her. I'll drive her."

"Don't you have a meeting this morning?"

"Yeah. I'll drop her off on the way. She's not up to taking the bus. But we have to leave soon, Span."

I didn't move.

Dad came and knelt next to the bed. "I'll drive you." He glanced at his watch. "Look, I'll drive you and have a word with your teacher. Span, please. Will you let us try to help you?"

I looked at his face, so full of worry. I needed to trust that he could help, that he could fix it.

"I want to change schools," I whispered.

"You can if that's what you need to do. You can. But meet me halfway here. Go to school. I'll talk to Mister…Mister—"

"Black."

"Mr. Black. But, Spannie, we've got to go."

There wasn't really time for breakfast, but my mother poured soy milk over a bowl of homemade muesli and gave it to me anyway. I tried to eat it while she shoved things into my backpack: lunch box, science textbook, wallet, keys, phone.

My father darted from his study out into the kitchen, laptop under one arm, manila folders under the other. He dumped them on the table and patted his pockets. "Where's my damn phone?" he asked no one in particular. Then he was gone again, back to the study. Katie appeared, earphones in, eyeliner smudged artfully. Dad returned, phone pressed to his ear. The three of us trooped out the door.

Katie slid into the front seat and switched the radio from AM to FM. I sat in the back behind Dad. He made another phone call. "Yeah, mate, I'm going to be late. I know, I know, nothing I can do. Got to drop my kids at school. Start the meeting without me, OK? I've got the Zurich stuff, just set up the projector. Stall them. Do what you can." He put the car into reverse and shot out of the driveway. He caught my eye in the rearview mirror. "It's going to be OK. We'll work it out. Katie, for Christ's sake, turn it down."

"Hey, if I'm going to get detention for being late, I'm gonna make it worthwhile."

Dad flung the car around corners, barely pausing at stop signs. He turned onto the highway and accelerated up the hill. The intersection of Johnson Street was at the top of the hill, at the crest. He moved into the lane to turn right. The lights turned yellow. His phone rang, and he reached for it at the same time he accelerated through the intersection. I don't know if he saw the truck come over the crest. If he did, he must have thought it would stop—but it didn't.

The sound of the truck's brakes. A shriek. Then a sound like an explosion on Katie's side, and we are sailing, sailing sideways. Time slows and I can see everything, every detail. Grains of twinkling glass rain like confetti. The car slides, pushed along by the front of the semitrailer, then it comes to a halt. Silence.

Nothing in the front of the car was where it was supposed to be. I thought at first that Katie's seat had somehow moved forward into the dashboard, but I realized the opposite had happened. It was like the front corner of the car had contracted in on itself. There was no room for Katie anymore. I didn't understand how she could still be there. Her face was turned toward me and her eyes were open. She looked frightened, but she didn't speak. There was blood on her forehead and cheek. It clogged brightly in her dark hair. I looked over to my father. His head was tilted back against the headrest. His eyes were closed. I started to cry and scream. I was sure he was dead. I reached forward and gripped his shoulder. Then I saw that his chest was rising and falling.

"He's OK, Katie," I said. But her eyes were closed. I said her name again and her eyelids quivered, opened. She blinked. There was a shallow, rasping sound in her throat. She was trying to breathe.

Someone was shouting at me. A woman.

"Are you OK? Are you OK? Oh shit. Shit!" She stood there, arms moving but not really going anywhere. A man appeared.

He pushed the woman to the side. She stood with her hands over her mouth, crying. The man went to Katie's door and tried to open it, but it wouldn't work. He ran around to my side and wrenched my door open. He leaned through and looked over me. "You're all right," he said forcefully. "You're all right! OK? Ambulance is coming. Can you keep talking to her?"

I nodded.

He pulled open my dad's door.

"Stay awake, Katie, stay awake," I said. Her eyes were still open and she was watching me, shocked. I talked to her while the man checked out my dad.

"Can you hear me, mate? Can you hear me?" he shouted. He looked back to me. "He's breathing well. Pulse is good. OK? Keep talking to her."

I did. Her eyelids drooped, like she was dozing, but I knew she could hear me.

There were sirens, building and building as they got closer. An ambulance and fire truck arrived with a piercing wail and I remember wishing they would cut it out. It was too much. Then the paramedics: one on Dad, one on Katie.

"What's her name?" he asked.

"Katie. Her name's Katie."

He put an oxygen mask over her face, talking to her calmly while he adjusted it. More sirens. Two more paramedics ran to the car: a man and a woman. There was a fireman with a huge pincher-like thing. They started to cut the door off. The paramedics were yelling about how they couldn't stabilize her. A paramedic left Dad and came to me. He put a neck brace on me and then an oxygen mask. He showed me a weird-looking thing like a padded back brace with straps all over it. As he slid it slowly behind me, he explained he would do up the straps around my chest and my head, and it would keep me safe while they got me out of the car. All I could think of was how it was a little late for that.

Then he and the female paramedic began to lift me out and I wanted them to stop, to leave me, because as they took me out, I couldn't see her anymore.

TWENTY-TWO

MONDAY. ANNE SITS opposite me, her elbow rests on the arm of the chair, propping up her chin. Long dangling strands of purple stones hang from her earlobes, swinging when she moves.

"Your mum phoned me this morning. Do you know why?"

I don't. She has never phoned Anne before. Since the accident, it's always Dad who calls the school if something's wrong.

"She said you had a fight. She was worried about you. She said she thinks you might be starting to remember what happened."

My head feels like one of those cannonballs you see in cartoons: heavy and thudding, with a wick lit, set to blow. I imagine exploding right there in Anne's office, blowing apart into little fluttering pieces. Settling like dust on the carpet.

"Are you starting to remember, Hannah?"

"It wasn't his fault."

Anne leans forward a little. I keep my eyes on my lap, where my hands are clasped, fingers laced so tightly that I don't know if I will ever be able to pry them apart.

"I'm sorry?"

"It wasn't his fault," I repeat a little louder.

Out the window, in the sky, a flock of birds twists and turns against the blue. They dive, climb, change shape together. So many tiny birds come together to form one large one. I wonder how they can keep their eyes open with the air rushing past them so fast. I wonder if it stings.

"OK. Do you think it was someone's fault?"

The birds switch direction, the head becomes the tail. "Not his." My voice is a whisper and I'm not even sure if I've spoken at all. "He was trying to help me."

I can't see the birds anymore. They are blurry and distorted, like I'm looking up at them from the bottom of a deep pool. I feel the first tear slide.

"Hannah. It wasn't your fault. You know that, don't you?"

"It was. I was a coward."

"You were not a coward, Hannah."

"I was the reason we were in the car. I was the one who was late because I didn't want to go to school. I was a fucking coward. I let them treat me like that. I was the reason we were in the car. And you know what's worse? She died and it all stopped. They—everyone here—they stopped everything."

Anne doesn't flinch, doesn't recoil or look at me in horror. Instead, she hands me a tissue. "The people who tormented you for so long suddenly grew a conscience. You didn't make anything happen. You didn't wish for this to happen."

There is snot and tears, and my head thuds.

"If I were stronger, Katie wouldn't be dead. It's that simple."

I wipe and wipe at my cheeks with shaking hands. My whole body feels tired, hollowed out. There is no energy left to try to stop the tears.

"I don't think it is that simple. But if you remember now what happened, you don't have to be assessed by a psychiatrist. You do have to stand and testify at the trial. They will ask you questions, and you will have to tell them what you remember because you'll be under oath."

I nod.

"OK. Look, I don't think you should be here today. I think you should go home. I'm going to call your mum. In the meantime, you can wait here. Is there anyone who you want to come sit with you? A friend?"

Josh enters Anne's office, hands in his pockets, shirt untucked. He looks around, eyebrows raised.

"Jeez, they give you the presidential suite, Jane? You know what this place needs? A flat-screen TV. Yeah, I can really see a TV there under the window."

Anne has given us both glasses of water and gone into her adjoining office. Josh sips his water, smacks his lips. "You know, I appreciate this, Jane, I really do. Shoulda seen Rourke. I swear, she was about to throw me through the window—then I got called out of class." He dips his head a little, looks at me intently. "You all right?"

I shrug.

He sighs. "And I thought I was effed up."

"You are."

He smiles, gives my arm a little shove. Then he takes my hand and squeezes it.

Josh carries my backpack, and we make our way across the school grounds, toward the front gates. Everyone else is in class, learning about ancient Rome or *The Great Gatsby* or the life cycle of plant cells. My hands are still shaking.

"Don't get any ideas about this, OK?" he says. "I'm not going to be carrying your stuff everywhere from now on."

"Least you can do. I got you out of class."

"Yeah, well. At least you haven't gone off on me for being a chauvinist. Had this girlfriend once who almost punched my head in because I opened a door for her. Swore I'd never be polite to a female again. By the way, you eaten anything? Like, this year? Looks like you're about to disintegrate. It's the only reason I'm brave enough to carry your backpack."

"Not really. It's not my strong point at the moment." We get to the front gates and he unzips his backpack and hands me a bag of corn chips. I try to eat one, but it feels like cardboard in my mouth. Josh watches me and there's a quietness in his eyes. Not pity, something else.

"You gonna be OK, Jane Eyre?"

I swallow, try to nod convincingly.

"'Cause I wasn't actually drunk. I meant what I said. I like having you around."

I feel like I could cry again.

"I'm a good listener, you know," he says softly. "Despite what they say around here."

My mum's car turns into the drive. She pulls up in front of us and gets out. She has brushed her hair and pulled it back. She is wearing lipstick. I see the moment she notices Josh and does a double take. He doesn't hesitate, walks over to her, and offers his hand.

"Hi, Mrs. McCann. I'm Josh, friend of Hannah's."

"Oh. Hello." She shakes his hand, gives me a sideways look.

Josh hands her my backpack. "Better get back to class. Hate to miss anything, you know."

"Sure," my mother says. "Thank you, Josh."

"Pleasure, ma'am. See you, Hannah."

I smile, overly aware of my mother next to me trying to work out who this guy is who shakes hands and calls women "ma'am."

———

Mum drives slowly out of the school. She keeps looking over at me.

"You tell me when you're ready to make a statement. I'll take you. OK?"

I nod.

She reaches over and brushes her fingers against my cheek. It's the first sign of affection she's shown me in I don't know how long. She wipes her face and I can see that she is crying.

———

Nanna and Grandad were there, next to my bed in the hospital. They were on one side, and my mother was on the other. When I opened my eyes, she was holding my hand, her head next to mine on the pillow, her eyes closed. When I woke up, she sat up and put her hands on either side of my face. She started to cry. Nanna explained that they had sedated me to reset my ankle and to calm me down because I was hysterical in the ambulance. I remember that, there in the hospital, was the only time I had ever seen Nanna without makeup and it seemed like such a strange thing to notice. I was in a room by myself and I thought that was odd. I felt there was a reason for it.

"Is Dad dead?" I whispered.

"He's going to be OK. He's in surgery," Nanna said.

"Where's Katie?" I looked at my mother.

Nanna patted my arm. "You should try to get more rest."

"Where's Katie? Mum?"

Mum couldn't speak. Grandad stepped forward and took my hand in his. I had never seen him cry before.

"Hannah, Katie died," he said softly.

"But I was talking to her—she could hear me. No. She's not. Where is she?"

"Love, she died when they were trying to get her out of the car."

I stayed curled up on the bed, drifting in and out of sleep. Every time I woke, I would think it was all a dream before the reality of the hospital room would chip its way in. Two police officers came in to speak with me, both women. Nanna and Grandad had left by then, but Mum remained, holding my hand.

"Hannah, we know it's hard. But we need you to tell us what happened."

I focused my gaze on a fine crack that ran down the wall next to the bed. It looked like a river might as seen from space: vast tracts of emptiness on either side.

"Hannah?"

"I don't remember."

"Tell us what happened leading up to the accident then. What happened that morning?"

"I don't remember anything from that morning," I told them.

"Really? Nothing at all?"

"Nothing at all."

They didn't leave it at that. They spoke to my doctor and the nurses. They came and visited me at home. I couldn't tell them anything.

It seemed bizarre that she could be killed so simply. Katie couldn't be killed by something as ordinary as a car accident. I don't think I really believed that she was dead until later, when I saw her body. Sometimes, I still don't—it just seems too strange.

I was released from the hospital two days after the accident. I was lucky. I had whiplash and a broken ankle. Nanna and Grandad came with Mum to take me home. As we walked out of the hospital, my mother broke down just outside the sliding doors.

"I can't leave without her," she said. "I have to take her home! I can't leave her in that cold room."

It was horrible. I felt like I wanted to vomit. The people standing around the front entrance, some in hospital gowns, some smoking, glanced at Mum and then quickly looked away. Nanna shushed Mum, and she and Grandad led us to the car. You couldn't tell Nanna was upset other than the tears that slid silently down her cheeks.

We went home and Nanna instructed Mum to take two of the sedatives she had been prescribed. The local paper was in the driveway. Grandad swiftly picked it up in the hope we wouldn't see the front page. But I saw the headline: *HORROR CRASH KILLS TEEN!* I felt angry that they had used such a cliché to describe what had happened, as if it were just another ordinary tragedy, comparable to every other story that had ever used that headline.

TWENTY-THREE

Now WE GET home and Mum doesn't say anything else and neither do I. It feels looser between us though. I go outside to the flat rock, and I sit there watching the tops of the trees. For the first time in a long time, there is no static in my head, no noise, just quiet—the type of quiet that comes after you have made a decision. After a while, I hear the back door slide open and I turn, expecting to see Mum, but it isn't. It's my dad. He leans on his crutch and hobbles stiffly down the stairs to the path. He keeps his eyes on the ground in concentration, and I can see the deep line between his eyebrows. I turn and look back up to the trees as he nears me.

"Hey, Spanner."

"Hi."

He lowers himself down onto the rock, sets the crutch leaning up against it.

"You're home early," I say.

"I think we're both a bit early today."

"Yeah."

"Mum phoned me… She said you feel you can make a statement." He pauses and looks up at the sky. "Whatever happened, Hannah, you tell them the truth."

"I will."

"I did something stupid, didn't I? I've been able to feel it."

I can't answer him. I just shake my head.

"Listen to me, Hannah. None of this is your fault." His eyes meet mine.

"I disagree," I whisper.

"Well. You're wrong. Look at me, Hannah. Tell them exactly what you remember."

"Can Nan take me?"

"To the police station?"

"Yes."

"If that's what you want, sure."

On Tuesday morning, she is at our house at eight o'clock with a fresh loaf of bread and a pot of homemade marmalade. She makes me and Dad toast for breakfast and instructs both of us to eat up. But I can't.

In the car, the radio is turned up loud. Nanna doesn't sing though; she just sighs a lot. And then she looks over at me.

"What a bloody wretched business this is."

I focus on pulling the breath into my lungs and letting it all out again. Like I'm swimming. We get to the police station and my hands shake when I open the car door. Nanna walks in beside me, chin up and shoulders squared.

Senior Officer Warner is younger than I remember her. Her brown eyes are carefully made up, hair pulled into a sleek bun. She greets us and gives me a smile like a doctor who's about to administer an injection.

"Hi, Hannah. Thank you for coming in today. We're going to go into the interview room. Can I get you anything? Tea? Coffee? Water? I can probably even rustle up a Coke if you want?" She speaks like a librarian, ushering us into a small room with a table and four plastic chairs. Nanna asks for two cups of water. When Officer Warner has left us, she shifts her chair closer to mine.

"I'm here," she says. "You're not on your own."

The policewoman returns with two plastic cups of water.

She sits down and moves her chair in close to the table, folds her hands on its surface. Her fingernails are perfectly manicured and I wonder if they come in handy when she has to arrest people. Although I can't imagine her arresting anyone.

"Hannah, I'm going to be recording this conversation. If that's OK with you, can you say yes for the tape?"

"Yes."

"Thank you. I'm sorry we have to ask you to do this. I can imagine it's very difficult, but the more information we have, the better decision the judge can make. I would like you to tell me everything you remember about the accident from when you first got in the car."

"OK."

Nanna puts her hand on my shoulder and squeezes it. I tell them everything.

The sky is dark with clouds when we come out of the police station, the air thick and humid. Nanna holds my hand and puts me in the car. When we arrive home, my father is on the back deck, leaning on the railing, gaze cast out over the bush. The trees bend and moan in the wind. I go outside to where he is, and the first few fat drops of rain begin to fall, speckling the baked concrete steps. He looks over at me.

"Hannah, I am so, so sorry." His fragility tears at me. You're not supposed to see your own father like this. I want to look away from him. He looks up at the sky, blinking in the rain that sweeps under the deck awning. He finds his voice again.

"Whatever happens, Han. It will be OK. It will all be OK. We will all get through it."

The only thing I have in my head is a picture of Katie, sitting there on my bed, crying over Jensen.

Thursday. I haven't been to the cemetery since Katie's funeral. It's behind a golf course, on a hill dotted with turpentine trees. As we walk through the headstones, I read the names and dates. There are a lot of loving and much-loved grandparents. Sometimes, there are two graves side by side—husband and wife. There are a few children, and when I read their epitaphs, I feel as though I am intruding on someone else's sadness, yet I can't help but look. There are some headstones that are so old that the writing has been eaten away by wind and rain, the things intended to remind us themselves faded.

Some graves have fresh flowers placed on them, even one that is twenty-two years old. There are a few with fake flowers: faded and brittle from the sun. Less maintenance, I guess.

My dad hobbles awkwardly over the uneven ground. Mum

is next to him, but they don't touch. When we reach Katie's grave, he lowers himself onto the ground. He kneels there on the parched grass, head bowed.

Katie's headstone is white marble with black lettering, and I can't help wondering if it's what she would have picked. I've heard people talk about graves as if they're talking about the actual person, saying, "We went to visit old Aunt Beryl" or whoever when they actually visited the grave. I don't feel like that. Katie isn't here. I don't know where she is, but she wouldn't be hanging around near a golf course with a bunch of old people.

There's a bouquet of fresh tiger lilies on her grave. Mum has brought purple tulips. She stands in front of the grave and looks at it for a little while. Then she puts the flowers down, leaning them against the marble.

"Some of her friends must have been here," Mum says. "We miss you, beautiful girl."

TWENTY-FOUR

PEOPLE BROUGHT US meals for a while after the accident. My mother and I ate endless frozen lasagnas and pot pies. Actually, "ate" is probably too strong a term. We defrosted them in the microwave and put them on our plates, that was about it. When Dad came home from the hospital, the meals stopped and it seemed strange to me. He was on crutches, his legs reassembled like a Lego set. Not exactly the picture of domestic efficiency. I can't help but wonder if there wasn't another reason people stopped cooking for us.

The funeral was held at the church attached to the school. It was packed with people. Everyone in Katie's class was there, half of mine too, crammed into the back of the church, overflowing out the door. I walked past them all with Mum and Dad as we went up to the front of the church to take our seats. The other students clutched tissues, sobbing and hugging each other. Most of them didn't even know Katie—people she wouldn't have spit on if they were on fire. There were students there who had hit me with spitballs and created Facebook pages in my honor. The Clones were especially dramatic; black eyeliner running down their cheeks, they looked like clowns from a slasher movie. I felt a touch on my arm as I walked past them. Tara and Amy were standing there with gleaming hair and sad eyes.

"I'm so sorry about your sister," Tara said. "You must be, like, so sad."

I didn't say anything.

"You should totally come sit with us when you come back to school," Tara said.

I walked away.

Before the service started, Charlotte's mum, Karen, came over to us with Charlotte trailing hesitantly behind her. Karen hugged Mum and Dad and then me, squeezing me tight.

"I'm so sorry, sweetie." She stood back. "We never see you anymore, Han. We miss you."

Charlotte stepped forward awkwardly. "Sorry about Katie," she mumbled. I wanted to slap her. Instead, I just nodded and turned away.

People said the service was lovely. Mum couldn't stand up—she sat in the pew sobbing while Dad held her hand. I listened to the prayers and the eulogy and felt numb, like I was watching a bad made-for-TV movie. Anything I did felt artificial: here is the grieving sister placing a rose on the coffin; here is the grieving sister handing the mum tissues; here is the grieving sister bowing her head in prayer. I was playing a bit part and not playing it very convincingly. Then the school choir sang "Stand By Me," and I could see Katie standing next to me making gagging gestures.

Afterward, the students made an honor guard and eight guys from her homeroom carried Katie in her coffin out to the hearse. One girl who I had never seen Katie with once was sobbing particularly loudly. I could feel Katie roll her eyes.

There was a wake in the church hall. I've never understood why it's called a "wake." Is it a last ditch effort to wake the dead person up? One last chance to make sure they are really sure about the whole being dead thing? "Good one, Katie! You really fooled us this time!"

The months after the funeral were silent. Time became stagnant when there was nothing left to organize.

I returned to school five weeks after Katie was killed. It was as long as I could stand being at home with my mother. She would sleep till noon, then wander around the house, red eyed and silent. The only break was when visitors came. They flooded in during the early weeks, bringing casseroles and cakes. I think we would have set a world record with the amount of cups of tea that were made in the two weeks after Katie died, either drunk or left to go cold next to the row of sympathy cards on the mantel. Gradually, the flow of people ebbed; they started to phone instead—until there was nothing left to say.

It was Nan who took me to school the first day I returned. She drove me in her pale-pink hatchback, rosary beads dangling from the rearview mirror. (She's not even Catholic.) I wanted her to drop me at the corner so I could walk up to the gate with no fuss and embarrassment. She wouldn't. It took everything I could do to stop her honking her horn in warning when we arrived. She pulled up to the gate and practically drove right through it. Faces looked up, eyes latched on. Nan glared at the other students like she wanted to attack them. "You can do this, Hannah," she said sternly.

I got out of the car and shut the door.

Eyes followed me up the sidewalk, through the front gate. I went into the bathroom. The chatter that echoed off the tiled walls stopped; the girls crowded around the mirror looked at me for a moment, then looked to the floor. I went to roll call and everyone was quiet. Mr. Black gave me a card, *With Deepest Sympathy*. It was signed by all the students in my class.

The Facebook pages disappeared. Nobody hit me with spitballs or pieces of clay. No one graffitied my stuff. It was like there was a force field around me.

―――――――

My mother has her hand on my shoulder. She steers me through the people who mill around in the lobby of the courthouse. Nanna and Grandad trail behind us. There are judges in robes, clutching to-go coffees. A woman in a slim black suit checks her lipstick in the reflection of a mirrored wall. Uniformed police officers talk in groups, heads bowed. A man in a tracksuit argues with a security guard. When we find the courtroom, it isn't what I was expecting: no polished oak paneling or high ceilings. Just a room with tables and plastic chairs, a raised bench at the front. Except for the wooden coat of arms, it's almost like a classroom or a really cheap church.

Officer Warner arrives holding a cardboard tray with two to-go cups. She hands me a hot chocolate and my mother a coffee. My mother's hand shakes so much that she can't hold it steady. "Thank God for lids," she says, and Officer Warner laughs a little, pats my mother's arm. A lawyer in a suit comes over and speaks with Officer Warner and my mother. I don't listen. I keep my eyes on a doorway to the left of the front bench. There is a shadow hovering there, and I wonder if it is my father. My body, my bones and muscle feel pulled to that doorway. Then a young guy with gelled hair and a baby face tells us we are to rise for the judge.

Nothing after that feels real. My father sits in a chair next to his lawyer. The prosecutor calls my name, and as I walk up to the stand, I feel as though the floor is moving beneath each step I take. I put my hand on the Bible and swear that every word I say will be the truth. The prosecutor is polite, not aggressive like they always are on television. She asks me questions. She asks me what color the light was when he drove through the intersection. If it was already red when the truck came through. I tell her it wasn't. I tell her about the phone ringing. My father sits with his eyes closed, tears streaming down his face.

The judge speaks about the impact the accident has had on our family, about the suffering and punishment already experienced by the death of Katie. She gives him a six-month suspended sentence. My mother is crying. I look to Officer Warner. She smiles at me. "He's not going to prison."

My mother and I sit at the dining table opposite one another. Dad has gone to bed, exhausted from the day. Nanna and

Grandad have filled our pantry and washed all the sheets on our beds. My school uniform hangs ironed in my closet. Mum wouldn't let them stay, and now we sit with a piece of microwaved lasagna on each of our plates. The fan ticks and ticks, pushing warm air around the room. My mother looks up from her plate.

"Do you want to go to school this week? It's up to you. You have to do whatever you feel helps you…"

"I think I will. If that's OK."

She nods, takes a sip of water from her glass. "You know, Hannah, we're both very proud." Tears trickle down her cheeks. She sniffs, wipes at them. "Sometimes, I think, my God, I'm not even here. You must feel like your own mother has been replaced by some…some impostor. I know I haven't done a good job of looking after us all." There is terror in her voice, in her face, and she looks at me pleadingly. "Hannah, I know this isn't fair to ask you, I know, I know." She clenches her eyes shut for a moment. "But, Hannah, was Katie awake? Did she say anything? I'm sorry, I'm sorry. I just… It's all I can ever think about, whether she was in pain…"

"She looked at me. She was looking at me. And I was talking to her. I said the stupidest things. I made a joke about her trying to be a vegan. So stupid. And I talked to her about this boy she was seeing."

"She had a boyfriend?"

"Jensen. He was wonderful."

"I didn't know that."

"She didn't want you to know. I was talking to her, and I could tell she could hear me, and then...then it was like she fell asleep."

I watch my mother. Her gaze shifts into the middle distance between us. She puts her hands to her mouth, closes her eyes, her shoulders shake. I don't tell her about the horrible rasping sound of Katie trying to breathe.

My mother wipes her cheeks with a tissue. She sniffs loudly, breathes as if she has just come up for air.

"Hannah, I love you very, very much. You know that, don't you? If you weren't here... I don't know... I don't think I could be here either."

"I know, Mum."

I stand up and clear our plates from the table.

The air in the café is cool, big ceiling fans whirl steadily. Most of the tables are empty. He is sitting at a chair by the counter, newspaper on his knee, an almost-finished coffee in his hand. He doesn't look at me but stands and walks behind the machine.

"What can I get you?"

"Hi, Jensen."

When he looks at me, his expression is almost one of fright. He takes a small step backward.

"It's Hannah. Hannah McCann."

"Shit. Sorry. You, um…" He shakes his head. "You look like your sister. I… Sorry. How are you?"

"I'm OK."

"It's really good to see you. Sorry to freak out on you. I just…" He runs his hands through his hair, shakes his head again. "You really looked like Kate standing there. Sit down. Here." He comes back around the counter, pulls a chair from a table. "Want a coffee? I'll make you one."

"Please. Latte, one sugar."

I sit down. When he's done, he sets the coffee in front of me, takes the seat opposite.

"It's really good to see you, Hannah. I'm not, you know, just being polite. I often wonder how you're doing. Especially the last week or so. I just… I can't believe it's been a year." He looks out the windows, to the street. "If I think about it, I get too angry."

"I get that."

He clasps his hands on the tabletop, hunches over a little, head dropped.

"I want you to know, Hannah, I never meant to…" His eyes

look up at mine. "I never wanted to hurt her. I really… She was wonderful. I'd never met anyone like her. I don't think I ever will again. But she told me she was older, Hannah. And I just felt… When I found out she wasn't even sixteen… I didn't want to hurt her. I just wanted to do the right thing. I really cared about her. I thought I should break it off. I didn't want to. She was so young. I thought we could wait a little while. I could wait a while. And you know, I was willing to do that. There wasn't anyone else. There hasn't been. And then she died… Shit, listen to me. She was your sister. You lost your sister. Who am I? Just some guy she went out with. I'm sorry, Hannah."

"You don't need to apologize."

"Well. We all need to apologize for something."

"Someone puts flowers at the intersection. All the time…"

"Yeah. That's me. I hope it's OK for you. Doesn't upset you?"

"It doesn't."

He takes in a big breath, then looks up at the ceiling, squeezes his eyes closed. "Can you stay a few minutes?" he asks me. "Just… Can we talk about something else, just for a while? I've got another two hours to go here and…"

"Sure."

"Good." A smile. "What are you reading at the moment?"

"Aldous Huxley."

"The light stuff as usual then?"

"Yeah, just the light stuff."

"Your parents know you read that?"

"They've kind of got other stuff going on. How's school?"

"Hmm. School. Kind of dropped out. Or 'deferred,' if you will."

"You dropped out? Why?"

"After Katie…I just couldn't get my head in the right place."

"You can't drop out. Do you know what I would give to go to college, like, right now? How bad is it? You have to read all the time and have intelligent discussions. Sounds horrible."

"Thought I'd work a little. Travel."

"You have to go back and finish."

"If you say so."

"I say so."

He opens the door for me and walks with me out onto the sidewalk.

"Come back, OK? Don't disappear on me. I want to know what you're up to."

"What if you're in Argentina or somewhere?"

"I will let you know if I'm going to Argentina. Just don't be a stranger."

TWENTY-FIVE

WE FOLLOW THE track down the side of the gully. Josh is bare-foot. The soles of my shoes slip on the rocks, and eventually, I give up, take them off, and carry them. The others follow us; the only names I know are Sam Wilks, Maddie, and Lola, but there are more. We carry plastic shopping bags of food: chips and chocolate and fancy cheese that Maddie insisted was worth paying ten bucks for. Sam has a six-pack of beer and Josh made a point to assure me we won't be binge drinking and going on a reckless crime spree like *A Current Affair* says we will. I would have been surprised if that was the plan because there's only enough for half a beer each.

Our voices and laughter echo around the gully. A flock of

cockatoos evacuates branches overhead, drowning us out in a chorus of screaming squawks. When we reach the bottom, we drop our stuff on the rocks by the creek bank.

Josh wades into the rushing creek. "Awww! Jeez, it's freezing!"

Maddie scoffs. "You're soft, Chamberlain."

He kicks water over her, then catches my eye. "You wearing your swimsuit, Jane? Hope so. I won't feel safe otherwise. You know, Jane here saved my life a couple of weeks ago. She completely jumped off the cliff."

"It's not really a cliff, Josh," I say. "Close enough though. I could have died."

"Wait," says Lola. "You did the whole drowning thing to Hannah?" She laughs and I feel the familiar dread building in me. Maybe this is the point it's revealed that everything Josh has done has been part of an elaborate prank. My brain lurches around, grabbing at every horrible possibility—it was a dare to see if I would have sex with him; he was going to film me having sex with him and share it on Facebook; he was going to wait until I had my clothes off and then burst into laughter while simultaneously Instagraming the whole thing; everyone was going to point at me and say, *As if, Hannah!*

"You are completely pathetic. You know that, don't you?" Lola says to Josh.

His cheeks flush red, and he splashes us both.

"He has a fantasy about being saved from drowning by a pretty girl."

"*Shut up*, Lola! I will kill you."

"Not if you die of embarrassment first."

I laugh. "Leave him alone."

"Yeah, leave me alone." He bolts off up the rocks that lead to the drop-off.

I wait until the others are all in the water before I strip off my shorts and T-shirt. I have a new swimsuit, a fifties-style polka-dot one-piece. I bought it on a shopping trip to Westfield Mall, which, for the first time, was not punctuated by a panic attack. I do my best not to think about it—I just run to the edge of the rock, squeeze my eyes shut, and let my body drop into the water.

ACKNOWLEDGMENTS

I could not do what I do without the love and support of my husband, Nathan. I must also thank him together with Marcella Kelshaw for their relentless enthusiasm for Hannah and her story, without which I would have given up long ago. Thanks also to Lauren McCorquodale for her insights into sisterhood—something I have no experience of—and her plot advice. You were the one who knew Hannah had to jump off that cliff that is not a cliff. For technical stuff to do with police and courtroom procedures, much thanks to Kelly Zorn for answering all my tricky questions. For technical stuff to do with paramedic work, a big thank-you to Dean Zorn.

For some reason, I keep writing stories that feature failing parents. This is in no way a reflection on my own parents, who have been nothing but encouraging and supportive. So many thanks to Kaye and George Bryan for being the parents they are. Thanks must also go out to all my parents-in-law: Tine Ten Kate and Ray and Jenny Zorn for babysitting so I can do my dream job and all the things that go along with it. Finally, a big thank-you to the people at University of Queensland Press, who have helped me along the way, especially Kristina Schulz, Kristy Bushnell, Michele Perry, and super publicist Meredene Hill.

ABOUT THE AUTHOR

Claire Zorn lives on the south coast of New South Wales with her husband and two small children. Her first young adult novel, *The Sky So Heavy*, was shortlisted for the 2014 Children's Book Council of Australia's Book for the Year for Older Readers and the 2013 Aurealis Award for Best Young Adult Novel and longlisted in the 2014 Inky Awards.